LENNOX

The Mavericks, Book 10

Dale Mayer

LENNOX: THE MAVERICKS, BOOK 10
Beverly Dale Mayer
Valley Publishing Ltd.

ISBN-13: 978-1-773363-00-4
Print Edition

About This Book

What happens when the very men—trained to make the hard decisions—come up against the rules and regulations that hold them back from doing what needs to be done? They either stay and work within the constraints given to them or they walk away. Only now, for a select few, they have another option:

The Mavericks. A covert black ops team that steps up and break all the rules … but gets the job done.

Welcome to a new military romance series by *USA Today* best-selling author Dale Mayer. A series where you meet new friends and just might get to meet old ones too in this raw and compelling look at the men who keep us safe every day from the darkness where they operate—and live—in the shadows … until someone special helps them step into the light.

Planning to meet his sister in Germany, but, when she's a no-show, Lennox has his first inkling that trouble has come home in a big way …

When his sister and her best friend go missing, Lennox is determined to find and to keep his only family member safe … and her best friend. They were both doctors, traveling the globe with the UN. Lennox was proud of his sister's accomplishments. He'd never tried to hide their relationship, thinking no one from Lennox's Navy SEALs past cared—or was still alive. Only now someone has decided to use Lennox's only family as a way to exact revenge.

Helena is caught up in a kidnapping of Lennox's sister, all designed to get back at Lennox—the most infuriating man she's ever met. And one she's cared for since forever. Now to know she was used as a trap to kidnap his sister and to take him out was the worst kind of punishment. But she *knew* this man. Knew him intimately—if only once—but also *knew* he was coming to rescue them, even if it meant losing his own life.

Lennox wasn't letting the only two women in his world be taken out without a fight, … especially one who didn't even know how he felt …

Sign up to be notified of all Dale's releases here!

https://geni.us/DaleNews

Books in This Series

Kerrick, Book 1

Griffin, Book 2

Jax, Book 3

Beau, Book 4

Asher, Book 5

Ryker, Book 6

Miles, Book 7

Nico, Book 8

Keane, Book 9

Lennox, Book 10

Gavin, Book 11

Shane, Book 12

Diesel, Book 13

Jerricho, Book 14

Killian, Book 15

Hatch, Book 16

Corbin, Book 17

Aiden, Book 18

Boxed Sets and Bundles

https://geni.us/Bundlepage

CHAPTER 1

LENNOX CUMMERBUND LANDED just outside of Munich, Germany. He was meeting his sister, Carolina, for a couple days, hoping to get that much time with her before he got called on a mission himself, having finished with Keane's assignment. As Lennox walked out of the airport, his duffel bag over his shoulder, he gazed around, looking to see if she had gotten in before him and was here to pick him up.

A couple days ago they'd made arrangements to fly into the same airport, roughly around the same time. He had her flight number on his phone but hadn't had a confirmation from her that she had managed to catch it. As he walked through one of the lengthy areas of the airport, he saw the computerized flight board above. He quickly checked her flight info. So she should have gotten in about ten minutes before him.

He sent a text her way, saying he would wait outside the front doors near her baggage pickup area. They could grab a cab and head to her apartment that she had here. She was a Red Cross doctor and traveled all over the globe. Breaks off together were hard to come by.

She was his only sibling, and they liked to touch base, if they could, at least once a year. When Lennox received no responding text, he frowned, wondering if Carolina was still stuck on the tarmac, but, even then, they were allowed to turn on their electronics again. He waited inside now, at the luggage pickup. Carousels rolled through for her particular flight. She should arrive here at any time, and, indeed, a crowd had showed up.

He scanned the faces but found no sight of his sister.

His frown deepened, wondering if she couldn't make it. He sent her yet another text; when that didn't work, he dialed her phone number, and his call immediately went to voicemail. Shrugging, he sat at the exit, watching as people came and went. Maybe she got in on an earlier flight, or possibly she was still stuck in whatever godforsaken part of the world she had been in last. He thought it was Somalia.

And given the connecting flights that she probably had to take, she could have been stranded anywhere. Usually she'd send him a message, if that were the case. He checked his email while he was here, but still he had no word from her. Now he was starting to worry.

"Lennox?"

His gaze shot up as he studied the tall dark-haired man in front of him. "Gavin?"

Gavin reached out a hand, and the two shrugged, shook hands, and half hugged in a typical bro manner.

"Damn, it's good to see you," Lennox said. "Odd place, but then, maybe not. I hardly recognized you. You're not in uniform, so you're not here on business?"

"Oh, I'm here on business," Gavin said. The smile fell off his face. "And I'm still in the military, just not the same unit."

"Ah. A lot of that going on. I'm here visiting my sister," Lennox said, holding up his phone. "At least I would be if I could find out what flight she's on or where she got stuck.

Her flight arrived, but she's not on it."

Gavin nodded, his expression turning serious. "That's why I'm here."

Lennox felt something inside him still. "Why?" He straightened his duffel bag at his feet as he glanced around. It seemed everybody suddenly moved slowly, as if only his world had sped up to the point where it all focused entirely on Gavin's face.

"We have reason to believe she's been kidnapped. Your sister, as far as I know, landed at this Munich airport and was snatched outside the terminal here. We waited until you landed to inform you and hoped we'd have more details by now. But we're still digging."

Lennox stared at Gavin in shock. "Seriously?"

Gavin nodded. "Come on," he said. "I've got wheels."

"Well, if Carolina's been kidnapped," he said, "we should take a look at this airport, where she was snatched."

"We're hoping to find her trail more effectively and more efficiently via the video feeds."

"*We?*"

"I'm part of the Mavericks team now."

Lennox nodded, then pointed at the airport behind them. "Then we should be heading inside to review their security feeds, awaiting intel before we book our next flight."

Gavin shot him a look. "We *are* securing a flight, but we're taking a military transport."

Lennox stared at him. "So I've been tagged for this mission to head up, or is this assignment just because it involves my sister?"

"Both," said Gavin. "In most military and even civilian cases, you wouldn't be allowed anywhere close to this op. But the Mavericks get to make the rules and have decided you're probably the best person to track her down."

"You're damn straight, I am!" Lennox said, swearing fluently. He threw the duffel bag over his shoulder and said, "Lead the way."

Within minutes they were in a nondescript car, heading out of the airport, moving through lanes and lanes of traffic as they navigated toward the main US base on the outskirts of Munich.

"Have you ever been on this base?" Gavin asked.

"Lots of times," Lennox said. "Most of the personnel probably still remember me."

"Right, you were stationed here for a while, weren't you?"

"Yes, and I was here for training several months at a time too."

"Good. Hopefully we've got some orders when we get there."

"I can do without the orders," Lennox said. His voice was hard. "I need intel."

"That's coming too."

"Who's running ground crew on this one?"

Gavin looked at him. "I have no clue. I'm not even sure I understand how all this system works, honestly. When they tagged me for this mission, basically because I was so nearby, I told them that they needed somebody with more Mavericks experience, and they just said, *This is how we roll.*"

Lennox thought about it, then nodded. "That's exactly how they roll," he said. "It wouldn't have anything to do with my Mavericks experience either. I just ran my first Mavericks mission with Keane," he said. "And I knew the next one was mine to head up, but I hadn't expected it to involve my own sister."

"I don't think the Mavericks expected this either," Gavin said.

"Do we know a reason why?"

"Not that I've been told."

"Nobody's seen her since then?"

"No, we're not sure who's behind this or why they were targeted."

"*They?*" Lennox pounced. "So it wasn't just Carolina?"

"Four on the same medical team," Gavin replied. "Your sister, another doctor, and two nurses."

"Which means Helena as well."

"I don't know Helena," he said. "Who's she?"

"My sister's best friend. They've been working as a medical team since forever," Lennox explained.

"Doctor or nurse?"

"Doctor."

"So three women and one man are confirmed on the team. The Red Cross is taking this very seriously."

"Of course they do," Lennox said. "They can't get doctors and nurses to work for them if they're being kidnapped randomly. Safety for them is paramount." Lennox paused for a moment. "How do we know they were kidnapped? Or are we just going on the basis that they didn't show up for their connecting flights?"

"We think your sister's medical team members were seen being marched into the back of a vehicle. No visual confirmation yet on the captives," Gavin responded. "The witness got scared when he saw the men were carrying weapons and decided not to report it for at least an hour."

"Did he describe the gunmen?"

"Four white men in military fatigues with machine guns."

Lennox swore at that. "Well, that doesn't help."

"No, the witness did wonder about the direction they were traveling, as the road led to another part of the airport. So it's possible they were flying the captives somewhere else."

"Which would be smart on the kidnappers' part," he said. "When you think about it, a lot of traffic occurs at a major international airport. That hinders our progress tracking them, as we have to delve through massive amounts of security tapes. Plus the kidnappers and their captives could easily have been flown elsewhere. But where? Why?"

"If only our witness had stopped and waited longer to see where they went, … but you know what the airports are like. The traffic comes and goes quickly."

"Cameras?"

"Yep," Gavin said. "The vehicle headed to the section reserved for private planes, but it only shows them taking that turn."

"And do we know anything about those private planes on the ground at the time?"

"No, we don't," said Gavin. "Outside of the fact that the terminal exists. However, the hangers we've contacted so far are not willing to hand over any security cameras."

"So hack into them," Lennox said harshly.

"In progress as we speak," Gavin said.

"If we don't know where or why she's been taken or who took her, how do we know where we're supposed to go next?" Lennox blew out a frustrated breath. "By going to the US base, we could be going in the wrong direction," he snapped in frustration. "That's a complete waste of time, if so."

"It will be, indeed," Gavin said, "but we're waiting on intel regardless."

"So, on to the military base, then—hopefully by the time the next naval plane leaves—we can hijack it to our new destination."

"That's the plan."

"Better be," said Lennox, muttering to himself as he stared at his clenched fists. With just his sister and him left in the family, the two were close, very close. The thought of her suffering sent shudders down his spine.

"Is your sister still feisty?"

"You mean, arrogant, snappy, domineering, and sometimes aggressive? Yes."

Gavin laughed. "Sounds like she can hold her own."

"She's had to," he said. "She hasn't had the easiest time climbing the ranks. She's had several incredibly sexist bosses and coworkers, plus an abusive ex-husband. Now that she's single and traveling the world again, she's learned that showing she has a backbone of steel and honesty can do her some good but can also do her some harm."

"True enough. But is she likely to keep her head in a scenario like this?"

Lennox thought about all the circumstances in Carolina's life and what she'd been put through already. "Yes, I think so."

"Good. What about Helena?"

"She'd shoot you in the balls just as soon as talk to you," Lennox said, his voice harder than he expected. He could feel Gavin's searching gaze, but he refused to rise to the bait.

"How long have they been friends?"

"From grade school," Lennox answered. "They determined they would be doctors a hell of a long time ago," he said, admitting his surprise at that. "I didn't think they'd make it, figuring their dreams would change as they got older, but they are committed to being doctors."

"Both married?"

"Both married guys named Peter. Both divorced. Both were in abusive relationships."

"Jesus," Gavin said. "A little too much twinning for me."

"They've always been that way. They were apart for a while, both working in distant parts of the country, keeping in contact via social media and Skype and the like. When they both came home around the same time with their respective Peters, they both married quickly, then kinda led separate lives again, neither one copping to their abuse yet in touch all that time, until their divorces happened within about six months of each other too. That had them getting reacquainted again."

"Seriously?"

Lennox looked at him. "Yeah, seriously wrong. But it did happen."

"I can't imagine such a life, but still that sucks."

"Well, they had each other to recover," Lennox said. "They were always the best of friends, and that didn't weaken throughout the marriages or the divorces."

"I'm sorry for both of them. Any children?"

Lennox sucked in his breath and shook his head. "They were both pregnant. Both of them lost their baby."

"Jesus!" Gavin said and went silent.

Lennox settled into his seat, wishing that he could forget about the trauma his sister had gone through. Or the trauma that Helena had gone through. Both of them had been pregnant early on in their marriages but about a year apart. And neither had known about the other's loss until they'd come together after the breakups of their marriages.

They'd both taken a beating somewhere around the time

of the miscarriages. He looked down at his still-closed fists, reminding himself of the beat-downs he gave both Peters. To this day he wondered how he had held it together enough not to kill those two sorry excuses for humans. Lennox shook his head even now.

He couldn't believe that his sister, who was so feisty and stood toe-to-toe over every argument, had let some guy beat her up. When he had talked to her about it afterward, she'd stared at him with tears in her eyes and said, "I don't know how that works. I'll yell at anybody who's abusive in a hospital. I'll protect every patient," she said, "but somehow I let my husband hit me."

She'd gone through all kinds of self-defense training afterward, plus assertiveness courses, shrink sessions, and had done everything she could to pull herself back together again.

As for Helena, Lennox had no clue how she had dealt with her recovery—other than her close relationship with Carolina. But Helena had been in a very rough foster care system for all her earlier life, so she must have learned how to cope way back then. Afterward, she had gone to med school on full scholarships. She was a brainiac, supersmart. But maybe knowing that she was finally loved—supposedly by Peter—had allowed her to let her defenses down, even when her brain was screaming at her that she was making a horrible mistake.

Lennox knew a lifetime could be spent on studying such a field, and still no answers are guaranteed to come up. He didn't know if Helena had done the same kind of assertiveness training that his sister had done; he hoped so for Helena's sake. This kidnapping though, it would be a rough go for all of them.

"Still amazing that the two are so close and that so much

synchronicity existed in their lives."

"I think they would have been quite happy to have skipped out on a lot of it though."

Gavin laughed. "No doubt. At least they both got out of a bad situation."

"Do we know anything about the other two people in the party?"

"One's a male nurse by the name of John Steadman, and the other is a female nurse, called Sasha Kempton."

"Is there any reason to consider this personal, as an act against the Red Cross, or just a political statement?"

"We haven't heard anything yet. We are doing a full rundown on all four of the kidnap victims."

"Well, I doubt your information will be any more detailed than what I already know about two of them."

"Hence why you're perfect for this job," Gavin added. "You know what? If this were a regular military op, you wouldn't be anywhere close to this."

"Oh, I would be," he said, his voice low and deep. "They just wouldn't have liked the way I made it happen."

"Right, still the same old Lennox then."

"Absolutely," Lennox said. "I'd have quit the navy and gone in myself, if that were my only choice to inject myself into this investigation."

"Well, the good news is, it doesn't have to happen that way."

Just then they entered the security at the base. By the time they were cleared and moved forward, heading toward the offices, Lennox was already on his phone contacting the Mavericks. Keane was on the other end. "Have an update on where my sister has been taken to?"

"We lost sight of them at the airport. No flight plans

were filed on the private planes."

"Do we have a satellite on them?"

"We do, but we haven't located them yet though."

"How long until we do?"

"With any luck, another ten to fifteen minutes."

"Okay," he said. "We're just pulling into the military base."

As soon as they parked, he hopped out, his phone in his hand, and tried to call his sister once again. With no answer, he quickly sent a text to Keane with Carolina's phone number, email address, and a couple other personal details. **Find her**, he added.

Keane answered. **We've got this. I'll have an answer for you soon.**

HELENA OPENED HER eyes and stared around the small cargo plane. She and Carolina were tied up, as were the other two members of their group. Somehow they'd been taken from a departure lane outside the airport at gunpoint and moved into the back of a small truck, then driven to a private airstrip, on another airplane even now. She had no idea where they were being taken or why. What did bother her was the half-military, half-mercenary–looking mix of males on board. So far there had been no sexual connotation, and, as a doctor, she knew her skills were highly valued, but her entire medical team had been taken. Why?

She exchanged hard looks with Carolina, who stared at her. Helena had taken a blow to the side of her head and was dealing with quite the headache. Then so had Carolina. Helena raised her eyebrows ever-so-slightly, silently asking

Carolina if she was doing okay, and Carolina gave her best friend the slightest of nods back. They'd always been very good at reading each other's thoughts, keeping track of what each other were doing and how they were feeling, so Helena was pretty confident that, although her best friend had taken a blow to the head, Carolina would be okay.

Helena glanced at the other two; John was sleeping. The kidnappers hadn't hit him at all. He was small, wiry, very efficient at what he did and hadn't put up much of a fight, so maybe that's why their captors had gone easy on him. Sasha, the fourth member, stared down at her feet, as if wondering about the state she now found herself in.

At the time they'd been accosted at the airport, they were all talking about their days off. Helena was heading with Carolina to Germany. Carolina would spend time with her brother, whereas Helena, who had a hard time being around Lennox, planned on visiting some other friends nearby. She would stay at Carolina's apartment because it was convenient and easy. They'd been friends for so long that sharing a space was just second nature. And it had been Carolina's idea that Helena come stay at the apartment. "You won't see much of Lennox. I promise."

Helena had snorted at that. "Anything is too much."

"You'll have to get over that," Carolina said. "He's not a bad guy."

"He rubs me the wrong way."

"And I've told you why," her friend had said in exasperation. "The two of you are so damn perfect for each other that you have to get past that initial almost hate-driven type of relationship you've got."

"And how will that improve anything?" Helena asked. "He's hardly somebody I want to spend time with."

"And yet you're attracted to him. You can't fool me."

"He's a healthy sexy animal," Helena said. "What's not to like?"

"So what's the problem?"

"He's more than a penis," she'd said, laughing. "I can handle the physical, but I don't think I want to live with the rest."

"And I think that's just because you're so damn much alike," Carolina had said.

"No, we aren't." Helena had been determined to shoot her friend down on that point.

"Yeah? Well, every time I ask him what's wrong with you, I get the same answer. Gorgeous body, gorgeous face, but you know, *I'd still have to live with her.*"

The trouble was, Helena *was* attracted to Lennox. And it was way more than just the physical. But she also knew that Lennox went through women like crazy, and she wouldn't be just another one among the many.

She'd been very particular about the men she hung out with, up until she got married. Then she had made such a shitty decision with her husband that she knew she couldn't trust herself to choose the right one. She knew Lennox quite well, especially after the number of times they'd seen each other, but she'd also thought she knew her husband.

Her husband had been tall, slim, almost that gentry-type male; she'd never thought such a beast would be under that smooth surface. Lennox was the beast on the outside; she could hope that a gentle male resided underneath, but she couldn't be sure, and she couldn't take the chance.

Her ex had taken his fist to her jaw, to her ribs, to her stomach. She was pretty damn sure that's why she lost the baby she carried at the time.

To find out Carolina had been hiding the same damn secret about her husband had been hard. They both wished that the other hadn't had to suffer as they had.

They figured each had a fifty-fifty chance of having a decent marriage, so why had they both ended up on the negative end of the scale? Carolina had devoted herself to her work and had ignored men, whereas Helena was still searching the world of men around her because she did want a family. Yet every time she considered another intimate relationship, she found herself drawing back.

She couldn't even look at the strong aggressive alpha males because all she could remember were the fists that kept pounding her into the ground. And, of course, the problem with that was, her husband looked the exact opposite on the outside—a compliant beta male. So she felt she couldn't trust any males.

If she didn't want children so much, remaining single suited her just fine. Being a doctor, she knew all about IVF and figured that could be the answer for her. But then, so many horror stories kept coming up in the news about that too. It was enough to stop her from moving forward.

And now she might not get a chance to rethink that choice.

She studied the two guards at the other end of the cargo plane. They sat, talking among themselves, their weapons turned casually in their hostages' direction. Still it's not like her team was any threat to the gunmen. The four who made up her medical team were tied up but not gagged and not likely to give their armed guards any trouble.

Both Helena and Carolina had martial arts skills and kept up their training, trying out new and more advanced techniques, but Helena couldn't imagine doing a whole lot in this scenario. These men outweighed her easily by one hundred pounds each. Regardless, all the gunmen had to do was pull a trigger, and that would be the end of her and the others anyway.

Except … guns fired on airplanes were not her forte. Would their guards even shoot their weapons on an airplane midflight? Taking out a window on an airplane sounded like a really bad idea—one that would probably kill them all from the sudden depressurization of the plane itself if not when crash-landing. Would the gunmen risk that? Can a bullet puncture the hull of an airplane? Does it matter the kind of bullet from the kind of gun?

Helena knew absolutely nothing about guns either. Her mission was saving people, not shooting them. But rifles? On an airplane? These weren't handguns. Or she guessed they could be machine guns, not rifles. Regardless, surely rifles and machine guns were more powerful than handguns and were capable of long-range shots, correct? To her, it seemed even riskier to shoot a rifle in an airplane in flight than to shoot a handgun. Shaking her head, she wished right now that she had access to Google.

Helena thought, if the gunmen were carrying those weapons more for show, then it would be the four of them against the two visible guards and any they couldn't see. Granted, John and Sasha might be worthless in this situation. So it would be Helena and Carolina against the guards. Given the abusive relationships she and her best friend had been through, and the emotional consequences, Helena would pit her anger-fueled adrenaline against either of those guys. She bet Carolina would too.

Then her head reminded her of her injury as a piercing slash of pain bounced around like an echo in her mind.

She leaned back, closed her eyes, breathing deeply through the agony, until she felt the intensity of Carolina's gaze. She opened her eyes to see Carolina nodding toward the men. Helena quickly twisted slightly so that she saw the two gunmen. Both had their rifles down and were showing each other papers or something as they exchanged various pieces back and forth. Was it their IDs?

Helena had no idea if their kidnappers had taken their luggage or if their baggage was still sat at the airport. The gunmen *had* taken the captives' wallets, purses, all their IDs, and their phones. So that could be the paperwork they were shuffling between themselves.

How much longer would this flight be? Her head throbbed once more, interrupting any more thoughts on her escape plans. Maybe it would be better to tackle her captors once they were on the ground.

Just as she thought that maybe this would be a flight that never ended, the pilot called back to the gunmen, and they started their descent. She glanced at Carolina to see the fear in her best friend's eyes. Helena gave her a reassuring smile. But how do you do that when your hopes were sinking along with the plane?

Helena closed her eyes again and prayed for help.

CHAPTER 2

W HEN THE PLANE finally landed, the gunmen snapped orders in English to their captives, lifting them roughly to their feet and ordering them to disembark. Helena slowly made her way down the stairs, their legs free and no gags. *We must be far from civilization*, Helena thought. *Or isolated among the kidnappers' people.* At the tarmac they were moved into a vehicle. She glanced around at the small airport and at the mostly flat geography around her, which meant that she could be anywhere in the world.

She sniffed the air, feeling a warmth that she hadn't expected. She turned toward Carolina, but her best friend shrugged, as if to say she had no clue where they were. Helena glanced at the other two members of their medical team and only received questioning glances in return.

As they drove off, Helena noted a couple street signs, but she didn't understand the language. That gave her a sinking feeling in the back of her throat. The language might have been something like Ukrainian. Maybe Polish? Maybe they were within a Soviet red block country? And, if so, why?

Although the laws were a lot more relaxed outside of the US, they could have traveled anywhere. So why here? They hadn't landed at an international airport. The kidnappers' options would have been unlimited if they had, but here, a small airport, fewer people watching. Fewer people to pay to not watch … And were she and her team any better off here—wherever *here* was—than in Africa, where there was almost no law? Where everything was available for a price? Then the Ukraine was likely to be the same too.

Her team didn't have their phones, although Helena had seen the gunmen checking them out, so their phones were close by. As long as the gunmen didn't break them, she had hopes of getting them back.

The drive ended rather abruptly as they were taken down a long driveway into what appeared to be some farming community. The vehicle backed up to a long metal building, and they were quickly unloaded and left inside the building in a large metal cage—resembling something made of a chain-link fence. She stared at the place in shock. A barred twelve-by-twelve-foot cage. She didn't know if it had been used for this purpose before or had been used to hold animals in the past.

"Bathroom?" Helena asked one of the gunmen.

He froze, glanced from one to the other, shrugged, and said, "Yes, just a minute." And then he went over to talk to the other man.

The man nodded, and they were each led to a small room in the same building and given a few minutes in there. She used the facilities in private, then barely had time to wash her hands and face before the door was opened again, and she was yanked out. As soon as they'd all had their time alone in the bathroom, they were led back to the cage and locked up again.

"Why are you doing this?" Helena asked in what she hoped was a reasonable tone.

But the men ignored her.

"We could pay you," she said hesitantly. One gunman

shrugged. And she realized money wasn't the motivator. Or maybe the other guy was paying them enough that they wouldn't be bribed. "Who is behind this?"

He looked at her, smiled, and said, in perfectly good English, "You're just a casualty." He pointed at Carolina and said, "She's the real reason you're here." And, with that, he turned and walked out.

LENNOX CONTINUED TO pace outside the main headquarters of the base, while Gavin passively watched his partner. Lennox's skin crawled to get into action. This waiting was not good for his mental health. This being about his sister made all his adrenaline rush through his body. When he got his hands on the guys responsible for this, … Lennox wasn't sure he wouldn't kill them all. He called Keane. *Again.* "Still no answers?" Lennox asked.

"Some," Keane said. "We're just figuring out why."

"Where is she?"

"Poland."

Lennox froze. "Seriously?"

"Yes."

Lennox shifted the phone to his other ear. And then decided it would be better on Speaker, as he spoke to Gavin. "This is Keane."

Keane calmly said, "Hi, Gavin. Back to your sister. Last we picked her up was in Warsaw at another private airstrip on the side of the main international one. Where her flight landed. We're still getting camera feeds off the airport itself, but it looks like she was down on the ground. We're looking for confirmation that they disembarked."

"Do we know if it stopped somewhere else first, before reaching Poland?"

"Always checking for stops," he said. "You know that. But we're working on it."

"So I'm heading to Warsaw then. Correct?"

"Yes."

"On it," he said, turning to Gavin. "We need to get moving."

The two walked inside the main office on base and quickly made arrangements and were then informed that the next flight wouldn't leave for another two hours. Lennox swore at that. "Is there no other way?"

The personnel quickly went through all the schedules but found absolutely no way to get into the Eastern Bloc country faster.

"Fine," Lennox said, pissed at the delay.

"It's still fast. Keep in mind she didn't arrive very long ago," said Gavin. "What? Two hours maybe, tops?"

"And now, with the delay here, we'll be at least four to five hours behind her," he said, shaking his head, his lips in a taut grimace, his pacing resumed.

"Again, not very far behind. We should get more intel before we arrive."

"I'm working on that too," Lennox said. He sat down in the small room, brought his laptop out of his duffel bag, and logged on to the Maverick chat box. **Need satellite on the Munich and Warsaw airports. I want video feed of the flights coming in. And I want all traffic cameras watching planes leaving the airports, around the pickup and departure areas as well.**

Immediately links showed up. **Glad you're on your laptop now**, Keane typed. **We've got all hands on deck.**

Still not enough, Lennox typed back. **We can't get out of here for two hours.**

With any luck, we'll have a more precise location for you to head directly to by then.

Not luck, Lennox typed. **We need to make this happen.** He quickly minimized the full-screen chat window on his laptop so he could take a look at the links. A distant image showed the suspect plane coming in for a landing at Warsaw. But the cameras were just ever-so-slightly not centered as he watched the passengers disembark. He couldn't see his sister, but a small male appeared on-screen. Maybe the male nurse?

Lennox brought up the chat box and typed **I need a closer image on this one.** He quickly took a screenshot and sent it. **And an ID confirmation.**

Will come back to you in a minute.

Lennox knew that the Mavericks ground crew were now hacking into other cameras at the airport, trying to get a better visual.

Five minutes later, Keane came back. **We've got this image so far. One of the team, I hope.**

Lennox brought it up, and there was his sister's best friend. **That's Helena. Any sign of my sister?**

I can't see her disembarking, no. They were flying together though, correct? This is taken from Warsaw.

According to our plans, yes. He kept going through the camera feeds, looking for a picture of his sister to confirm that she was there. Just then the ID on the male he'd requested came back as the nurse John Steadman.

Good, Lennox typed. **Two confirmed.** He caught an image of a third female and got her name confirmed as well.

Sasha Kempton, nurse.

Okay. That established three out of four. **Now I need confirmation of my sister.**

Not until the transport vehicle had been captured on camera leaving the airport via one of the smaller airstrips did one of the security cameras pick up Carolina's face in the back seat of a truck. He immediately typed **Four confirmed.** And Lennox gave Keane the license plate and the picture with his sister in it. **Track that.** He sat back, looked at Gavin, and said, "That confirms all four were taken together."

"And Warsaw has been confirmed, so that's a good place to start," Gavin said, nodding at Lennox.

"It's a shit place to start," Lennox said. "Money buys you everything there."

"Good," said Gavin, "because we'll need weapons. The kidnappers had firepower. We'll need the same."

"Do you have a contact?"

"No," he said, "not in Warsaw. You?"

Lennox thought about it and shook his head. "No, so we need to find one." Lennox quickly texted Keane but didn't get an answer right away. Impatiently Lennox waited, and then Keane came back with a phone number for Lennox.

Weapons?

Anything you need but black market. No names, no countries, no affiliations, just money.

We'll need cash.

It'll be there in your vehicle when you arrive.

Good. I want to hit the ground running.

Make that running, not shooting. Remember the law in Poland as a little on the left too.

I don't care if it's left, right, or center, Lennox answered. **They've got my sister. You know I'll erase that country if they do anything to stop me from getting her back.**

Hardly subtle, Keane responded. **Remember. Stealth in, stealth out.**

You remember that, Lennox typed. **You guys brought me in on this. I'm not exactly known to be subtle.**

You can be when you need to be, Keane typed. **And, right now, you need to be.**

Why is that?

Because we think it's a trap.

He sat back, but Keane didn't say anything else. Lennox looked at Gavin. "They think it's a trap."

Gavin replied immediately, "Now that's interesting."

"Isn't it?" Lennox said. "But what kind of a trap?"

"I love that chat box," Gavin said, "but we need more answers."

"The trouble with being fast to respond," he said, "is when we can't get enough answers to set us free to just do this damn op."

"True. But we're on it," Gavin said, and the chat came back.

Almost immediately more information flowed. The vehicle his sister rode in was a rental. The company that rented it was a shell company, which the Mavericks were trying to track down for more details.

Waste of more time, Lennox thought. He highly suspected that, given the level of professionalism behind this kidnapping, the shell company's ID had been stolen, or the shell company's credit cards had been hacked, and still there wouldn't be a direct tie between the shell company and the real mastermind behind this kidnapping. **Ransom note?**

None.

So they aren't after money. Sex? Revenge? Power? Intel?

Trap. **Have you tracked a direction?**

North, but that's all so far. We're still running through the videos.

Lennox checked the time. They would be leaving soon. He quickly tapped in, **We'll be in the air in twenty. Or at**

least boarded.

When you land, we'll have more for you.

You better. And he quickly shut down his laptop. He looked at Gavin. "Are you ready for this?"

"Yeah, first stop is getting the vehicle, and then we need to get geared up."

"Vehicle is waiting on us already. So is the money, and now we have a contact for the weapons."

"That's good news," Gavin said. "So we need food, and we need rest."

"There won't be any food on this flight," Lennox said. "So we'll have to grab that as soon as we land."

"I guess what we need now then is to get some sleep."

"Not a whole lot we can do otherwise, so we'll sleep on the flight," Lennox said, but he probably couldn't sleep and knew just more sitting and waiting midflight would eat away at his insides. His sister was not the most patient person he knew. Obviously he wasn't either. It's one of the reasons she made such a great doctor. She was driven to help others.

At one point in time, she had considered Doctors Without Borders but had opted for the Red Cross because they headed out to some of the more dangerous areas where doctors were desperately needed. Lennox had been all about her getting a practice in suburbia, and she'd laughed her head off at him. "Me? No, not happening. That'd be like me telling you to go get a job as a bookkeeper at a retail store."

Something he knew he couldn't possibly do either. They were both very similar in their adventuresome spirits and even more so in their protective natures.

He wanted to fix the world, and she wanted to fix the people. They were both fools for thinking they could do either.

CHAPTER 3

S ITTING STILL FOR hours already—before in the gunmen's airplane, then in the truck, now in this cage—Helena tried hard for patience, but this whole situation was wearing on her.

By the time they'd spent a few hours in the cage, seemingly all alone, the team had opened up enough to talk a little bit.

"Anybody have any ideas why?" Carolina asked.

"No." Sasha's tone was terse.

So far they hadn't spoken much because they were all concerned about somebody coming in and telling them off, but they appeared to be alone now. They'd been offered no food, no water, and only the one trip to the bathroom. Nobody seemed nearby where the hostages could call out if they did want something.

Helena expected to see several of the men with machine guns hanging around, but they must feel that their prisoners were well secured here. She got up, paced their cage, before coming back to the gate on their cage and its simple lock. She studied it. "Anybody any good at picking locks?'

Carolina snorted. "Really? Us? Not likely. If Lennox were here, that'd be a different story."

"Well, it's Lennox we want to see," a man said, stepping through the entranceway of the long metal building. A man stood in front of them, tall, more Swedish looking than the others so far. Maybe German was a better description, considering where they were, but then it was hard to determine his accent. He had a big ugly scar across his cheek and some burn marks on his neck.

"Lennox?" Carolina asked with a frown. "What's this got to do with my brother?"

"Everything," he said. "You're the bait. The rest of these people are just here to keep you compliant. It's Lennox we want."

Carolina and Helena exchanged hard glances, and Carolina spoke up. "What do you want to see my brother for?"

"A little payback for his betrayal," the man said, his hand going up to his neck. "He owes me."

"Well, not that we want to get in between the two of you …" Helena said quietly, "but what are your plans for us?"

"Depends on whether Lennox behaves himself or not," he said. "You can all go free if I get Lennox," he said with a laugh. He waved his hand. "Sorry about the lack of hospitality. These certainly aren't the most comfortable cages, are they? Though Lennox knows all about cages too. He's done enough intensive mind warfare training to understand the psychological effects of being in a cage."

Carolina and Helena exchanged confused looks, followed by shrugs.

"I'm sorry. I don't know what you're talking about," Carolina said quietly. Her voice low, almost contemplative, she said, "I haven't heard much about his missions, so I'm not sure what happened between the two of you."

"He hurt me and mine …" the man said. "That'll never go down well in my book."

"Have you contacted Lennox to let him know we're here?"

He laughed. "Hell no. I can't make it too easy for him. He's on his way. I know that for sure. You guys were taken from a very public spot, so he's backtracking now to find you. We can't make it too complicated, and we can't make it too easy. But never forget that it's Lennox who we truly want, so, if you guys behave yourselves, then you'll be released unharmed."

Something Helena completely didn't believe. "Is there any chance of food?" she asked. "We traveled a lot getting here, and most of us didn't get to eat before we left."

He looked at her for a moment and then shrugged. "Sure," he said. "I'll get them to rustle up something for you." He turned and walked back out.

She looked over at the others.

John and Sasha stared at her. "You asked for food?" Sasha said. "How about letting us go?"

"That's not something he'll do," Helena said quietly. "So I looked for something he might be willing to give."

"Besides, we need food for energy," Carolina said. "No point in starving ourselves and being so weak we can't go anywhere if we do get the opportunity."

"And Lennox?" John asked.

"My brother," Carolina said. "He was a Navy SEAL, until he started some new job recently, only I don't know the details."

"And next you'll say that he doesn't betray others," Sasha said, her voice hesitant, and yet her tone held obvious contempt for Lennox.

Helena glanced at her. "Lennox is one of the most honorable men you'll ever meet," she said. "The only reason he'd have hurt this guy or someone close to him is if there was a damn good reason for it."

"But it sure explains why this guy's pissed."

"He can be as pissed as he wants," Helena said. "It won't change the fact that Lennox is pretty damn smart."

"And you're expecting him to come here and rescue you? Both of you?"

"All four of us, yes," Carolina said. "That was a guarantee as soon as we were grabbed."

"Which is, of course, why this guy grabbed us," Helena said. "Unfortunately this isn't good."

"Why?" Sasha asked. "Carolina's brother can just come in, and they'll grab him and release us."

Helena looked at Sasha. "Do you think it'll really be that easy?"

Sasha's face closed down. "The guy said he would."

"So he did." Helena walked over to where Carolina sat quietly on the floor and joined her. "But you know talk's cheap, Sasha. Let's see what these guys do when the time comes."

Just then the guard walked in, and he carried a tray.

Helena hopped to her feet and asked, "Is that food for us?"

He nodded. "There's lots of it, just not much variety."

"That's fine," she said. "Thank you. We also need liquids. Water would be good."

"I'll bring some water," he said.

As she watched intently, the guard held his rifle pointed at them, pushed open the gate to their cage, and said, "Everybody stand back."

As they all obediently moved to the opposite wall, the tray was placed on the floor, and then the gunman backed out. As soon as they were locked up again, the guard said, "Now you can eat."

Helena walked over to the tray and took a look. She counted at least two buns apiece and some sausages, plus a big bowl of potatoes. Only one fork. She looked at the others. "Anybody else hungry?"

"Doesn't matter if we are or not," Sasha said. "As Carolina said, we need food."

"Indeed." Helena reached for a bun, opened it, popped a sausage in, and started to eat. She then made another sandwich to-go. Helena walked to the back of the cage and sat down, handing Carolina one of the sandwiches, but she shook her head, then winced. "No," Helena said, "you need food."

Glaring at her, Carolina grabbed the sausage in a bun and said, "My head hurts. My stomach's queasy. And I'd rather have vegetables."

"We can't do anything about your head or your stomach here. Sorry. As for the food, it doesn't matter what you'd rather have," she said blandly. "This is what we have available, so you'll eat it."

With a heavy sigh, Carolina followed through, and Helena glanced around, all four of them sitting with one sausage and a bun in hand.

Two armed men—the same guard and the same scarred man—came back with four bottles of water, but they could pop them through the bars without opening up their cage again. Helena hopped up, popping the last of the first bun into her mouth, collecting the bottles. Then she handed them out to everybody. "Thanks," she said to the scarred man, who seemed to be the leader of this group.

He nodded, and both turned and walked out of the

building.

Helena eyed the massive bowl of potatoes on the tray and the one fork, then looked around to the others and asked, "Anybody want any?"

Carolina immediately shook her head, her hands going to her temples immediately. "I don't," she said. "Potatoes aren't my thing."

Helena looked at John; he nodded. "Go ahead and have some," he said. "There are lots." She picked up the bowl and ate until she was full, then passed the bowl and fork off to John.

She wasn't sure where her appetite had come from, but she also knew her blood sugar could drop, and she'd suffer then. She planned on getting along and playing nicely with their kidnappers and waiting for Lennox to arrive. She had no doubt he was on his way. One thing she knew for sure about Lennox. When you didn't want him, he was always around the corner. And, when you did want him, he was still around the corner.

Only he wasn't hers to want.

WITH THE VEHICLE rented—in Lennox's name, since this was an obvious setup, and he wanted to acknowledge that from the get-go—he and Gavin were back on the road. However, on all missions, the guys wore gloves, even now in a vehicle clearly rented for him. It was a SEALs rule that had carried on into the Mavericks. It was a good rule. Gave the SEALs and the Mavericks the ghostlike quality of slipping in and back out again that they desired.

Gavin drove, while Lennox found the briefcase under

the front passenger seat. He quickly went through it: one sheet with some addresses, lots of money, and two handguns. He looked at the guns, frowned, and said, "I wonder if we'll need those to get the rest of the weapons."

"I wouldn't be at all surprised," Gavin said. "Nothing's easy over here."

"I haven't done much in Poland. You?"

Gavin shook his head. "No. Russia, yes, but I haven't been here before."

"Well, we are where we are," he said. "So let's get to it. I need a full arsenal before I go in after my sister."

"Did anybody ever come up with any intel as to why?"

"No," Lennox said, "and that bothers me. There should at least be a ransom note, even if just as a diversion or to start the bargaining." He checked with Keane and asked again, but still there had been no communication from the kidnappers. "So why?" he asked Gavin.

"That's the question, isn't it? Why your sister? Was it random or directed?"

"I feel like it's very directed."

"I do too," Gavin said. "So how many enemies do you have?"

"You mean, how many enemies does my sister have?"

"Good point," he said. "That's possible too. Is she that argumentative?"

Lennox laughed. "No, but she's fiercely loyal," he said. "I'd say the ex-husband is probably her only real enemy."

"Would he do something like this?"

"I doubt it," Lennox said softly. "If he did, I seriously misjudged him. I was pretty damn sure I'd scared the shit out of him, and he would never even be in the same country as my sister."

"Sure, but maybe he's in Poland?"

"Last I heard he was working out of Quebec."

"But maybe that's changed?"

"Time to find out." He sent a message off to Keane, who came back with a reply five minutes later.

He's still in Quebec. Showed up for work this morning.

"Would he have arranged this from a distance?" Gavin asked Lennox.

"Not if he had any clue I would be involved," Lennox said. "And, if it involves Carolina, I'm involved. I made it very clear what I would do to him if he ever hurt my sister again."

"Then it's not likely him then," Gavin said with a note of satisfaction. "I'm surprised you left him alive."

"I am too," Lennox said. "Thought for sure I'd kill the bastard. He did time, and he's still facing other charges. But he's working hard to keep his nose clean now, last I heard."

"What about other women?"

"No confirmation on that, but, had I heard even a whiff of anything like that, I'm pretty sure he knows I'll come around snooping, so he'll keep it on the straight and narrow."

"I hope so, for his sake," Gavin said.

"I don't know about that. I hope the bastard crosses the line," Lennox said. "Then I can take him out. One less abusive male on the planet sounds good to me."

"What about you? Enemies? Personal? Work?"

"Same as you," Lennox said, leaning back, closing his eyes. "Probably at least half a dozen, if not twice that."

As he sat, reflecting, a couple missions came to mind. One had gone bad, where another SEAL had been compromised. Another one, where a soldier had died from friendly fire. The shooter had been doing a training exercise. He'd turned and hit a couple of his unit. Several of them had been injured, but one had died. The deceased's family had accused the rest of the team because they hadn't protected their son.

But they had, from external threats. Just no one had seen the internal threat coming.

There'd been missions where Lennox had had to turn in a team member because he had betrayed their country. Lennox wasn't proud of the fact that he had worked with these traitors, but Lennox sure as hell wouldn't let one go out on more missions and endanger more of his friends and teammates.

"There's always one or two unexpected wild cards, isn't there?" Gavin said.

"Always," he said. "You do your best but …"

"Right," he said. "So anything else? Anything personal? Any married husbands angry that you have been screwing their wives?"

"Not my style," Lennox said. "Single and available is the only direction I travel."

"Maybe," said Gavin, "but women don't always tell the truth."

"Isn't that too damn sad?" he said. "But, yes, agreed."

"Got it," Gavin said, "but we do know one thing for sure."

Lennox looked at him. "What?"

"Somebody did this. And that somebody is pretty damn serious."

"I know," Lennox said. "We'll find the bastard. You can count on that."

CHAPTER 4

HELENA'S SITUATION WAS getting old very quickly. Once they'd eaten, everybody more or less crashed in various corners of their prison for at least an hour or two.

Helena sat in her corner, her head against the back of the steel cage, wishing for a bed or a pillow. But she'd gotten food and wouldn't push their captors' hospitality. She could ask for so many other things in life. Carolina was nearby. As Helena looked at the others, the two had distanced themselves from her and Carolina. They would blame Carolina no matter what Helena said to defend her best friend. She didn't know very much about John and Sasha. They appeared to be trustworthy workers and decent people in hospital settings; that's all she'd cared about so far.

Of course now they were under stress, and their very survival had been threatened. That would change everything entirely. What Helena didn't know for sure was how long they'd hold up. She already knew what Carolina was made of. The same as Helena. Nobody goes through the abuse and the beatings that these two women had gone through without understanding a lot about who they were on the inside.

They'd taken more than they should have. They both knew that, but neither had reached a breaking point or turned around and killed their attackers. She often wondered if whether maybe she would have been better off if she had. In theory, it would have been a lot easier to move forward and to forget the nightmares. She always held on to that fear that her ex-husband would show up again, but so far he never had.

Carolina's ex had had a visit from Lennox. Helena had often wondered about asking Lennox to do the same with her ex, but that would mean crossing the line the two had drawn in the sand. *After one very heady kiss.* She almost smiled at that. Lennox had been pissed, and the kiss had been more about the ultimate punishment at that time, given their near-hatred of each other—or maybe more about competing with each other for Carolina's attention? Regardless, that kiss had just been a byproduct of his temper, but it had quickly flared into something way past that. So Helena already knew that they were both trying to avoid igniting that short fuse which was always present between them.

Besides, she didn't want anything to do with men at this point; Lennox was safe as long as she didn't get too close to him. She already knew that, if she did, the two of them would burn up the sheets come hell or high water, and everybody else would turn to ash if they tried to stop them.

Carolina's low voice interrupted Helena's thoughts. "Are you okay?"

Helena smiled down at her friend. "Sure am. We've been in worse scenarios."

"I feel like suddenly we have a room divider in here," Carolina added in a low voice, deliberately not looking where the other two had huddled together.

"Sure. We're to blame. Remember?"

"You mean, I am," said Carolina, never afraid of stating the truth.

"By association me too," Helena said. "Don't worry about it. It is what it is. We will get out of this."

"Only because of Lennox. Do you think he'll get taken?"

Helena knew that a flippant answer wouldn't help right here, right now. She thought about the man with the steely gray eyes and his linebacker build and the pantherlike movements that made him a deadly predator of the night. "It'll take a tank to bring him down," she said.

"No," Carolina said softly. "Bullets will do it too."

"We've seen a lot of men get up after being shot multiple times," she reminded Carolina.

"I know. It's not the kind of work I like to do anymore, but you and I have both seen our share of gunshot wounds. I know it can do a lot of damage, but I also know many men who survived."

"Lennox will know it's a trap. He won't come alone," Helena said. "He's too smart for that."

At least in her heart, she hoped he was. Yet, with his sister as one of the kidnap victims, how would Lennox react to that? He was as impatient as his sister. Plus he had quite the temper. Could he pull it together to let his mind overrule his emotions? Helena hoped so. Otherwise Lennox could be the ultimate victim here.

Well, one of them. Carolina had been through enough already. The last thing she needed was to lose her brother, her only family. She'd been talking of nothing but seeing him this week. It was essential to her that they continued to meet, not just for a meal but for several days on end, where they could relax and talk. Helena understood Lennox offered another perspective and helped keep Carolina grounded, and the bond between them was the strongest she'd seen between two siblings.

Anything that kept Carolina in good shape and moving forward with her life was enormous. Carolina's pregnancy had ended with that last fight with her ex. She had left him immediately. It had been the final straw. And, of course, she'd spun into depression after that. She'd always wanted a family. Carolina and Helena had both talked about wanting children at some point in their lives. Maybe they both had jumped into those relationships because they thought they were getting too old to have babies, and maybe life was running past them. They were in their early thirties now. And time was marching by, without either woman in any current relationship, so having kids looked like a long ways away from where Helena stood.

Helena had felt that time pressure to have children a little more than Carolina had. Yet it was still there, always just that piece missing from both friends' world that Helena knew would come, but later. Now it would be that much later.

"How long do you think before he shows?" Carolina asked, obsessing over Lennox as usual.

"Well, as far as staying in this very uncomfortable cage, I hope he will be here immediately," she said. "But who's to say?"

"I need to sleep," Carolina murmured.

Helena glanced down at her friend, worried she'd been sleeping a lot since she took that blow to the head. "You sure your head's okay?" she asked, leaning closer and brushing the hair off the wound.

"The head's nothing," she said. "You and I both know we've taken worse."

Helena glanced over at the other corners of their cage, where the two were lying down, their heads together, but each lay alongside the cage, far enough away from Helena and Carolina to not overhear their discussion. That pair didn't know anything about the two women's histories. "Maybe," she said, "but we shouldn't have to again."

"*Shouldn't have to* doesn't make a damn bit of difference when we're caught in the middle of this."

"I know." That brought her anger rising. Helena swore she'd never again get caught in a situation where she would be reduced to a punching bag. Instead here she was. … And who knew what the gunmen had planned for them. Talk of letting them go was cheap. … Their actions were what counted. No, she wouldn't think like that. Lennox was coming. He might not come for her, but he sure as hell would come for Carolina. Helena just had to hold on and wait.

LENNOX STOPPED AT the entranceway to the weapons storage unit, as the breath almost sucked out of his chest.

"Quite something, isn't it?" Gavin murmured. "And who gave us this guy?"

"Keane sent me the address," Lennox said; he pulled out his phone and quickly sent Keane a text, asking him where they found this place.

An acquaintance of Levi's.

"Well, everybody knew Levi or at least anybody who'd been a Navy SEAL knew of Levi. And Ice. It was hard not to. And, if they had a connection like this, well, makes sense to check it out."

A man stood waiting nearby, holding a clipboard. "I don't have all day," he said testily.

"Got it," and they reamed off their list. Lennox grabbed a flat cart and collected items off the shelves. By the time they were done and had paid the bill in cash, the briefcase had a significant dent in it. But it was all good. They loaded up the vehicle and left the parking lot, Gavin driving again.

Lennox shook his head. "Already have two tails on us. Which is damn obvious in this neck of the woods."

"What's it look like?" Gavin asked, glancing in the rearview mirror.

"Well, it looks like our friendly arms dealer plays both sides. He'll take our money and promptly give us up to the locals within minutes." Lennox sighed. "He gets paid twice for each gun deal."

Gavin shot another look behind them. "But they're not advancing on us."

Lennox fired off a text to both Levi and the Mavericks central command. "Probably just reporting our current position to the kidnappers. I doubt they will engage."

"You let Levi know?" Gavin asked, with a head tilt to Lennox's phone.

Lennox nodded. "Levi will handle it in his own unique way. And now … we have to ditch this vehicle soon," Lennox murmured.

"Already in progress," Gavin said. "We'll get to the next town and switch up the rentals."

"I'd suggest ditching the rentals and just buying something cheap on the side," Lennox said. "The kidnappers, courtesy of the locals, will already have our license plate, our faces, and they now know that we've got not only cash but a lot of weapons."

"Movement behind us. One vehicle jumped in front of the other. Not aggressively but way too obvious. Do you think these locals are coming after us? I count two in each truck."

Lennox turned to look out the back windshield. "Well, they'd be a fool to try. They know we're armed, and they must also realize we know how to use our weapons," he said. "But all that doesn't mean they don't have a secondary business going on right now, where they take out trouble-makers."

"Which, by the very nature of what we just did, counts us as troublemakers," Gavin said with a nod. "I got no problem ditching our ride," he said. "We're probably better off to change wheels every town anyway." They came into the rental lot, and the two following trucks drove right by.

"Well," Lennox said, Gavin by his side, watching their tails until they were out of sight, "this one road seems to be the only path from this town to the next. They'll be waiting for us there."

Gavin nodded, returned the vehicle, grabbed all their gear—including all the firepower now packed in an extra duffel bag—and headed out to rejoin Lennox, still in the parking lot. "Any more friends following us?"

Lennox shook his head. "Out here, a tail can be seen so quickly. And I doubt the locals have the money for drones or have hackers who can tap into satellites."

"Yeah, but," Gavin added, "the kidnappers might. The guy arranged for air transport of the victims. That couldn't have been cheap. … Or he has friends in high places."

They shared a knowing look, and Lennox repeated, "Trap. Yeah. I know."

"Where do you want to go?"

"I'll head into that restaurant over there," Lennox said. "We need food, and we need wheels."

"You order the food," Gavin said. "I'll take care of the wheels." Then Gavin took off, leaving the duffel bags for Lennox to tote around for now.

Lennox didn't even ask questions; he walked in, the heavy duffel bags in his hands, found a booth at the back, dropped the duffels under the table, and sat down. As soon as the waitress arrived with menus, he awkwardly ordered coffee and studied the food options as well. The translation app on his phone was a godsend in these situations. When she delivered the coffee, he ordered the special of the day times two, thought about it a second longer, and got two big meals to-go. He chose meals that could be eaten cold, big sub sandwiches, and several other dishes along that line. Also a refill of his coffee and a second cup. The waitress looked surprised but quickly wrote everything down and disappeared.

He sat here with his phone, wishing he could pull out his laptop but didn't take the chance of attracting any more interest. He was an obvious foreigner in this rural area. Many people in the restaurant gave him a critical once-over before resuming their meals. Lennox could feel their gazes on him every once in a while thereafter.

So the laptop wasn't a good idea here. Then he realized it didn't really matter because they likely didn't have any internet here. Cell towers were few and far between out here in farm country. He checked in with Keane to let him know where they were. Then asked, **Got me a location pinpointed yet?**

Give us two more minutes.

Lennox snorted at that, hung up, and set his cell phone off to the side. But he had to admit, so far—with everything that he'd been involved in with that chat box, between

Keane's mission and now this op of Lennox's—the Mavericks chat window had been a gold mine as far as resources went. He didn't know how many Mavericks were working on the back end, but Lennox knew this command center position right now was filled with like the seventh or eighth man who had done prior missions, and these were the only ones Lennox knew about. So he figured the Mavericks could easily gather an eight-man team, ready to go at a moment's notice. He pulled the phone toward him again and typed, **Are Gavin and I the only ones on a mission currently?**

    No. Kerrick and Griffin are off in Africa.

    Any connection to my case?

No came back the answer instantaneously.

Lennox pulled his coffee toward him and took a hesitant sip. And then smiled. It was thick, intense, black, and damn-near scorched his throat all the way down. *Perfect.*

He sat back with a sigh, rotating his shoulders and his neck to ease some of the tension there. They were fully equipped now, which helped on these overseas missions where air travel was involved, as that was always an issue, making sure that they had what they needed and without all the red tape involved with a by-the-books military op. Not that the Mavericks couldn't get some help from the US Navy or other branches of the military if and when needed. The Mavericks maintained a symbiotic relationship with their SEAL brothers for sure.

Now if only Lennox had a location on his sister.

His phone buzzed; he pulled it forward to see a link. He quickly clicked on it and saw the kidnapper's vehicle that had been at the Warsaw airport. It was driving through the town he was currently in. The time and date stamp said it was four and a half hours earlier. That wasn't bad. They were gaining a bit on them.

Stay on the same highway. You've got three more towns to go through to catch up to the latest surveillance we have reviewed to produce this bread crumb trail on the kidnapper's vehicle.

Time frame on locating their final destination with the captives?

We still don't have that intel, but we're damn close. So, when you're done eating, start driving.

Lennox stared as the waitress returned with large plates. He dug into his, even before she left. He knew the folly of not having enough fuel to run on. And that wouldn't happen today. More than that, he didn't know if his sister and the others in her group were struggling with a lack of food either. As soon as he ate half his fries, his phone went off again, and there was a map, and he saw the three towns marked with dots. **Those three are confirmed sightings?**

Yes, still working on the one after that.

They go off the grid?

Yes. Now we're searching via satellite.

Lennox kept eating, and, when he looked up, Gavin walked toward him with a smile on his face. Lennox motioned at the food.

Gavin sat down, surveyed the plate in front of him, and said, "Now this is what I call a meal." He picked up his knife and fork and dug in. Ten minutes later both had polished off their massive platefuls. When the waitress came back with the to-go bag, she stared at the empty plates in surprise.

Lennox looked at her, smiled, used his phone then said, "We were hungry."

They got up, and Gavin grabbed both duffel bags this time, while Lennox grabbed the takeout and walked up to the cash register. The woman never said a word, just rang up the order. When he saw the amount, he paid cash for it, smiled at her, and walked outside to meet up with his partner.

"I could have used a take-out coffee," Gavin said.

"If you want one, go back and get it," Lennox said.

"Nah, we've already got enough attention."

"Even the best of us," he said, "have to eat and drink."

"I know, but it still feels like everybody's staring."

"We're Americans. I'm sure they are."

"No way to be subtle out here in the wide open spaces, is there?"

"No, not at this stage, and we don't need to be. We've got three more towns to go through by the time we're done heading into the next district," he said. "The kidnappers have gone to ground. That's when we'll have to go incognito."

"Good enough," he said. Gavin led the way to a small pickup truck. They stowed the duffel bags in the back of the bed and hopped into the front seat. As Gavin started the engine, Lennox asked, "Did you pay cash for this one?"

"Well, I caught somebody trying to steal it," he said, "so I persuaded him that he didn't need to keep it."

Lennox laughed and laughed. "Well, we'll have to leave it somewhere on the side of the road. Be even nicer if the guy stealing it in the first place left his fingerprints here."

"We've both got gloves on, and the kid didn't."

Lennox chuckled. "Well that's a twist, isn't it?"

"I figured it would work. We'll have to switch it out soon anyway."

"Maybe not at every town now. I don't see any more tails."

They kept driving the truck for another forty minutes.

They'd already passed the next town and were in the middle of the second.

"Time to change vehicles."

Gavin shrugged.

"Maybe a double-cab truck this time, enough to handle six of us?"

Gavin nodded. "I'll see what I can find in the next few minutes."

Luckily, ten minutes later they were in their new wheels and back on the road.

"One more town to go." Lennox's phone buzzed again, with the one-word text, **Close?**

Not close enough, he typed. **We're coming into the third town.**

Got it. And the chat box disappeared. Lennox pocketed his phone and said, "They still haven't got a final location."

"How big is the area?"

"Last seen in a parcel about twenty square miles," he said. "Lots of farms, old homesteads," he said. "They could be anywhere."

"Twenty isn't bad though," Gavin said. "We've hunted with way less information and a much larger area."

"Isn't that the truth?" Lennox admitted. He and Gavin had done many missions together when they'd both been Navy SEALs. And both had come to the end of the road where they knew it was time for a change.

Lennox had never in his wildest days imagined even more black ops though. And this one was different in so many ways.

CHAPTER 5

HELENA GROANED AND shifted her position again. Part of the problem was the lack of a floor. The cage rested on the hard-packed dirt. Although it could be worse if there had been bars on the ground in this cage too. That would never be comfortable. How was the cage was secured to the ground? A quick check at the four corners and on both sides of the gate confirmed her fears. Steel rods inserted at each point were probably buried at least six feet into the ground. *So no lifting up one side of this cage*, she thought. Even if it could work, with twelve-foot-long sides, she'd have to get help from Sasha and John too, which was not likely.

Doubly frustrated now, she tried kicking up some of the earth to make a little bit of a pillow, but that didn't help. She rolled over on her back again and stared up at the ceiling. This building was a sizeable machine shop, one of probably a thousand of them around the countryside. How could anybody find them in this nightmare? But she knew better than to doubt Lennox.

What had Lennox done? Or rather, what did this guy think Lennox had done? The guy had an obvious tell; he brushed his scarred neck whenever he had talked about Lennox. But she knew, if it had been a mission that had gone bad, well, it would have been gone bad for Lennox too. Right? And he had no burn scars that she had ever seen. And

Carolina would have mentioned that, if he had had some serious injuries. Just because this guy had been burned in some event from the past, that didn't mean that Lennox was to blame for this guy getting hurt. ... That was a pretty strong causal accusation.

Lennox wasn't the kind of man to do shit like that without a good reason. And what did *betrayal* mean to this burn victim? If it meant that this guy was caught stealing, and then Lennox turned him over to the authorities? Well, so be it. Because, in that case, hell yeah, Lennox would do no less. But then she would as well. That's the way she rolled—straight up, straight forward. Everybody else and their little side trips into the gray areas of life weren't for her.

That's why Helena did well at her career. They went in, they did the job, and they got out. Unfortunately, it also reminded her that there was an awful lot of gray in life and it just brought all that shitty marriage stuff back again.

She glanced down at Carolina, seeing her eyes closed and her deep breathing. Helena shouldn't be worried about her friend, but there was something about her five-foot petite stature that made everybody look at Carolina as if she were a child. But Carolina had a steel core and a heart of gold.

Now Helena wasn't much taller at five-four, but those extra four inches seemed to make a lot of difference. In many ways, they wore the same clothes. Helena was a little bustier and of course a little longer, but that length was more in her legs, whereas Carolina had a longer torso. They often played around with each other's tops and sweaters and even some of their dresses and skirts, borrowing them when needed. Wouldn't it be nice if they were doing that right now? It sure beat sitting here as a prisoner.

Helena would need the bathroom again. She winced and

shifted her position to see if that would ease her bladder. But she was already lying flat. When she stood, it would get even worse. She sighed and then called out softly, hoping to not disturb the others. "What about a bathroom trip?"

A gunman immediately stepped in from the open door to the building, confirming her suspicion that they weren't ever alone. He nodded and asked, "Just you?"

"Yes," she said, gently getting to her feet. "The others are asleep."

"You can't sleep?"

She shrugged irritably. "No, I'm finding the ground a little too hard for my old bones."

He made a scoffing sound. But, in truth, she'd taken enough blows during her lovely abusive marriage that she found it hard to lie in certain positions now. Her guard led her to the bathroom. After relieving herself, she opened the door so he saw her; she turned on the water and washed her face and hands, then bent her head down and took a long drink.

"Are you out of water?"

She nodded. "Yes, the bottles all disappeared with the food."

"Of course, with potatoes and bread, you need water for those." He stepped aside, pointed behind him at a bucketful of ice water and bottles nearby, and said, "Grab another bottle."

She hesitated and asked, "May I take one for each of us?"

He nodded.

Helena pulled out four bottles from the bucket sitting there, and she walked back to the gate of their cage. The gunman unlocked it, let her in, and then locked it back up again. She sat down with the water, opened one, and had a long drink.

Sasha opened her eyes, saw the water, and asked, "Is there more?"

Helena tossed her a bottle and said, "One for each of us." She threw another one and said, "Give that one to John when he wakes up."

Carolina rolled over, groaned, and said, "Man, why aren't we in a five-star hotel?"

"We would be," Sasha said, in a hard voice, "if it wasn't for you."

"That'll hardly help the situation," Helena said, her voice in a carefully neutral tone. Sasha wasn't making friends with her accusations. "None of us knew this would happen. It could just as easily have been somebody you knew."

Sasha shrugged, took a drink, and then laid back down again. "But I don't know anybody who would be in a situation like this."

"Well, now you do," Helena snapped.

Sasha looked at her and frowned.

"You're already in a situation *like this*," Helena added, "so now everybody in your sphere knows somebody who's been in *situations like this*."

At that, Sasha shot her a disgusted look, closed her eyes, and rolled over.

Carolina laughed. "You don't need to defend me. You know that, right?" she asked.

"Maybe not," Helena said, "but nobody needs to be blaming anyone right now."

"But it makes people feel better," Carolina said.

Her best friend had taken a whole pile of psychology courses after her divorce to try to understand not only her husband's behavior—which both Carolina and Helena did more or less understand—but about Carolina's lack of responses, why she had taken the abuse. The two best friends had discussed that issue many, many times. This wasn't the time for another discussion now, but at least her education gave Carolina a chance to understand why Sasha was acting the way she was.

For Helena, she didn't give a shit; she just wanted Sasha to stop all these unproductive verbal attacks.

Carolina and Helena heard a commotion outside the building, and then two gunmen stepped inside, one of them the scarred man from before. They glared at the four prisoners, walked around their cage, checked to make sure that no loose bars were found and that nobody had come inside. "Did you see anybody?" the scarred man snapped at her in English.

Helena answered, "No, I haven't seen anybody but the one guard and you."

The scarred man glared at her, as if searching for the truth, then gave her a nod. "Better not. If you aid in your escape," he said, "we'll take that as a mark against you, and we will shoot you the next time."

She took a long, slow breath, trying to reach for some control, so she didn't snap at him. "We're trying to be cooperative," she said calmly.

"No point in *trying*," he said. "We have the upper hand. You are our prisoner, so you'll do what you are told."

She didn't say anything, just stared at him, her gaze flat.

He snickered. "You don't like that, do you?"

"I doubt anybody does," she said, once again reaching for some serene calmness as she searched for anything that might get them released. "Lennox should be here soon, I gather?"

"I hope so," he said. "I don't plan on feeding you for too long."

She winced at that. "We do eat a fair bit, don't we?"

"You do," he said, "but that's all right. We're okay for a few days. After that, if he's still not here, we'll shoot you." And he turned and walked out.

Beside her, Carolina whispered, "*Shoot* us?"

"Yeah, but whether that was a scare tactic or not, I'm not sure," Helena said. She looked over to see tears in Sasha's eyes. "Take heart," she said. "It won't get that bad." Sasha stared at her. Helena saw the vulnerability on the woman's face.

"I don't know this Lennox guy," Sasha said. "I don't even know for sure that he's coming."

"Well, we do know him," Helena said, nodding toward Carolina. "And he is coming. The problem is, these guys know it too, and they're waiting for him."

Sasha nodded, her long hair drifting in the dirt, but she didn't seem to care. It wasn't a high priority at the moment. "Is he the kind of person to make it past those armed guards out there?"

"Absolutely," Helena said, thinking about Lennox. "If anybody can help us, he can."

"I hope you're right," Sasha said, "because we won't survive if he doesn't." And she rolled over, away from the two women, and ignored them.

Carolina nodded beside her. "She's right. Our kidnappers don't have the tolerance to wait for a few days. If this isn't done with by tomorrow, you know what'll happen."

"Maybe not," she said.

"Count on it," Carolina whispered. "These guys don't have any intention of playing around. If I'm not a big-enough lure to bring in Lennox, they won't waste their time and resources with guarding and feeding prisoners. They'll shoot us one by one until we're all dead."

Helena had to agree, but she didn't want to even talk about it.

Still, the commotion got her hopes up that Lennox had arrived. But now, since no gunfire had immediately erupted or no bombs went off or no truck on fire broke through a weak spot in the walls of this shop—what she considered Lennox's style in her mind—she decided it was not Lennox-related at all. Probably some wildlife in the area. Or just jumpy gunmen outside, seeing every moving shadow as a two-legged threat.

She had to trust that Lennox was coming. She knew his relationship with his sister was something that Lennox would bend over backward to save. What Helena didn't know was whether anybody would get hurt in the process. There were four prisoners. And any number of armed guards. Plus Lennox wasn't stupid enough to come in here unarmed. With all that imagined firepower, Helena knew it would be just too damn easy for one of them to get shot accidentally. The last thing she needed was to have anyone here die because of their own rescue attempt.

"WE NEED INTEL," Lennox snapped into the phone.

"I know," Keane said. "We're still looking."

"They couldn't have completely disappeared off the face of the earth."

"No. They didn't. We found signs that the vehicle went toward a farmhouse, then drove across the neighboring land.

But some black zone is out there. Yet we picked up the truck on the other side, and it appears to still have all the same people in it."

"Anything like that's an anomaly," Lennox said. "Tell me where it disappeared in the first place."

"I'll send you the GPS coordinates," Keane said. "Remember though. It isn't necessarily the final destination."

"Maybe not, but we'll start there, and, while we do, you'll keep the Mavericks working hard to find out exactly where they've ended up."

"Yes." And they hung up.

Lennox explained what had happened to Gavin.

"That's odd. I wonder if a big repeating station is here or if some power plant is sending off weird energy that's causing a glitch in the satellite feeds."

"Possibly. Let's take a drive out there and see." The GPS coordinates were not very far up ahead. When they took the left-hand turn, they saw other tracks ahead of them. "Well, somebody's been through here recently."

"Exactly. But it's anyone's guess who."

When they got to the spot, the dot on Lennox's phone buzzed and beeped. "Okay, my phone doesn't like this location at all."

"No, but as you can see,"—Gavin pointed out a big transformer station off to the side—"we never really understand the effects from these big power plants," Gavin said, "but everybody knows there's a hole in some areas because of them."

"And having this here means what though?" Lennox studied the area, realized the tracks continued, and said, "We might as well keep driving and see if anything suspicious is here."

"Alternatively," Gavin said, pointing to a hill, "we can go up there and take a look at the bigger picture and see if we can see anything of interest below us."

"Let's do that first, then follow the tracks if need be," Lennox said. A few minutes later they crested the top of the hill, parked, and hopped out with binoculars to take a look around. "Lots of small farms, little villages dotting the countryside," Lennox said. "I'm not seeing anything indicative of our missing people."

"No, I'm not either. I think we're too far away."

"Where do the tracks go from here?"

Gavin pointed them out. "They're coming around this hill and going down again. A road of sorts cuts through there. I think the power plant skewed the videos."

Lennox nodded. "Enough buildings and outbuildings are along here for any number of prisoners to be kept." He motioned to the barns, machine sheds, garages, even small houses, and what looked like a couple warehouses. "We're not short on places to search, and we're wasting time, so we need to make sure that we narrow it down as much as we can." Lennox assessed the area in front of them and said, "Probably got a good ten-mile area here. That'll take time to search on foot."

"True enough but we can hit almost every one of those buildings within the next couple hours."

"Maybe, but we should have a shorter time frame than that. Once we're moving around and checking out places, we're not foolish enough to think we won't be seen, not considering how many places we have to hit. The kidnappers will get word, and they'll be waiting for us."

"Hell," Gavin said, "they're already waiting for us now."

Lennox nodded. "I know it," he said. "And, of course,

that's what this is all about. It's a trap."

"Which is why we have to be smart," Gavin said. "I get that you want to go tearing in there after your sister. But it's *you* who they want."

"*Me* they can have," Lennox said, his voice icy hard. "But they don't dare touch my sister."

Gavin smacked him lightly on the shoulder. "We'll find her," he said. "You know that."

And Lennox nodded. He knew that. But the ultimate question remained. Would they get there before these assholes hurt her or even killed her? It depended on whether they thought she was a sound bargaining chip because, if Lennox got there and found her dead, he'd make sure that not one of them walked again. Hell, he'd be happy if not one of them breathed again. But he'd have to see just what went down first. If the kidnappers fought, they gave him a perfect excuse to take them out. And, if he saw anybody in any way involved in the kidnapping, well, that was good enough for Lennox to retaliate in kind.

The two men made their way back to the truck and drove down the hill to the small village. Just as they reached the first property with a massive farm, a barn, and a tractor machine shed, Lennox saw half a dozen people moving big machinery around and stacking up hay inside the barn. "This doesn't look like a good option."

"Too noisy, too many people, no visible guns," Gavin agreed. His phone buzzed at that point. He checked out the message. "*Keep going one mile. You should come upon a right turn.* The Mavericks lost sight of them there."

"Why?"

"A blink in the satellites as they connect to the next one, and it didn't catch that signal. *Be careful.*" Very quickly they hit the spot. They got out, walked on foot, studying the area. "Well, here's fresh tracks," Gavin noted. "I suggest we drive ahead to that pullout and the couple little tourist signs for that river, and we head back on foot."

Lennox didn't want anybody to have any idea they were coming. But, of course, everybody was waiting for them. Parking the vehicle, they quickly disappeared into the tall grass and bushes. They came along the neighbor's side, keeping an eye on the property in question as well as the one beside it. By the time they made it to the far side of the properties, Lennox saw multiple buildings, but there was no sign of anyone. He frowned, hunkered down into the brush, made himself a small area where he could lay down and use his binoculars, and peered through them. "I'll scan the east side. You take the west."

"Got it," Gavin said as he backed up to Lennox, facing the opposite direction and protecting his partner as well.

"People," Lennox whispered.

"How many?" Gavin asked.

"I see four men."

"Armed?"

"No. Not a one of them."

"Well, what are they doing then?"

"Good point," Lennox said. "They're just standing around and talking, near the opened double doors, yet inside that machine shop."

"So, are any weapons anywhere near those guys?" Gavin brought his binoculars around to search the same area.

"Not that I can see." Lennox shifted his binoculars, studying the next closest building in the area, a temporary shed—one of those metal half-circle-looking things that were put up fast and easy and usually reasonably priced. And they would hold everything from hay to equipment, and some had even been converted to housing when needed. There were rarely any windows on them in the back, like this one, although there was a window in the small rear door. And a window would help, but it was a long way away for Lennox to make a run like that to check if anyone was there. When he found his sister and her team, he planned on getting them out immediately. No return trip needed.

"Ten o'clock," Gavin whispered.

Lennox shifted to the left, checking out his ten o'clock. One vehicle and one man. And what was different about this one was he had a rifle on the hood of the truck in front of him, while he lit a cigarette. Lennox studied the weapon. "Nice piece of weaponry there," he murmured.

"Expensive," Gavin said.

"Absolutely. And in good shape. Not a spot of rust anywhere." Meaning that guy looked after his weapons, which meant he used them a lot. Lennox watched as the gunman had a smoke, walked around, studying the sky, then the woods around him. He never looked once in their direction. He continued to explore the rest of the area. "He doesn't appear to be guarding anything," Lennox said, his gaze zipping back to where the other men stood inside the machine shop. No one appeared in or around the shed.

"No," Gavin whispered. "But if there's one gunman …"

CHAPTER 6

"SO WHEN WILL your brother get here?" John asked. His tone held a sense of overwhelming despair, as if he didn't believe that Lennox would really come.

Helena looked at Carolina, who was lying with her arm across her eyes. Her knees were bent, relaxed, but Helena doubted her best friend was asleep. And she didn't bother answering John's question. So Helena glanced at John and shrugged. "We have no way of knowing if he even knows yet that she's missing."

He stared at her in surprise. "Well, didn't the kidnappers send a ransom note?"

"I don't know if they did or not," she said. "I don't know what they've done to alert Lennox to the problem."

John stared at her, frowning. "And here I was assuming the guy was already on the way," he said, turning around in the cage, his arms wide. "How long do they expect to keep us in here?" he cried out.

"As long as necessary," she said, her voice calm as she tried to get him to understand the situation wouldn't have an immediate resolution.

"This is not where I want to be," he said, getting more and more agitated. He pivoted and shook the bars. But the cage didn't even budge.

She saw his body jolt as he tried to force the cage to do

something. "John, calm down," she said cautiously. She hadn't seen him lose it before, and he was basically calm and even-tempered and had a ready smile for everyone. At least under hospital conditions.

He turned to look at her, and clearly their situation was tearing into him. "I can't stay calm!" he said. "I want to go home. I want to spend some time with my family," he cried out. "Why are they doing this to me? I didn't have anything to do with whatever her brother did."

"None of us did," Helena stated. "Including Carolina. It's about her brother, whether he did something or not. It's not about her."

"It's the same thing," he roared. He came over to stand beside them. Not sure what his intention was, Helena slowly stood protectively over Carolina. "She's already been hurt physically by the kidnappers," she urged John to caution. "Let's not add any more trauma to her stressed system."

"She's stressed?" he said, staring at Helena in disbelief. "What about me? What about Sasha? We didn't have anything to do with this. You two are always joined at the hip, so it's fine if the kidnappers keep you. This has nothing to do with us."

"I don't think the kidnappers particularly care who is here," she said coolly, as she stood here, feet planted apart, her hands ready to stop John from attacking Carolina, if that's what he thought he would do next. "They had a plan, and they didn't ask us for permission."

He stared at her for a long while, and then his shoulders sagged. "Look. I get that you're not responsible," he said in the most persuasive of voices. "But surely you can ask the guards to release us." And he motioned at Sasha, who was now looking at them hopefully and then at him. "Once they realize it's got nothing to do with us, I'm sure they'd let us go."

"I don't think they're gonna let anybody go right now. Not before they get what they ultimately want. After all, having four hostages is an advantage over having just two," Helena said, raising her palms in John's direction. "But you can always try asking them yourself, when they come back."

"When are they coming back?" he asked, running his hands up and down his face, pinking his skin with the effort. "I need to go to the bathroom."

"I don't know, John. Why don't you call out and ask one of the guards to come and take you to the restroom," she said in a reasonable tone, not quite trying to humor him but wanting to keep him a little more balanced than the upset man she saw struggling to get free. "When I called them earlier, they let me out to go to the bathroom."

He looked at her sideways. "But maybe you're special."

"I'm not special at all," she said, her fatigue obvious in her tone. "Just call out and tell them you need to go to the washroom."

He looked at her once and then walked up to the gate and called out, "Is anyone there? I need to go to the bathroom."

Almost immediately one of the guards stepped forward, took one look at John, and nodded. The gunman walked over without a sound, unlocked the door, let John out, keeping one of his guns pointed in his direction, and quickly relocked the door. He led John away to the bathroom.

As soon as they were out of sight, Helena sagged in place.

"You can't stop him forever," Carolina murmured.

"I know," she said, "but I'm hoping I can stop it for a

little bit longer."

"Stop what?" Sasha asked belligerently.

But Helena just stared at her. Because this was precisely what Carolina was talking about. It was a case of not having the others turn against them. And sometimes when people turned against each other, they got a whole lot more violent too.

"We just want everybody to get along, so we can get out of here peacefully," Helena explained.

"Well, we're not gonna get along," Sasha said. "Why would we? Just like John, I know that we don't belong here. You guys are to blame for this."

Helena could feel Carolina stiffen at that. "*To blame?*" Helena repeated curiously, trying to keep her tone still even and low. "Do you believe that?"

Sasha looked momentarily confused, and a whisper of sorrow appeared on her face for what she'd said, but then she immediately stiffened her shoulders and said, "Well, if anybody's to blame, it's you guys."

"We didn't have anything to do with this," Helena said. But she knew that her words would fall on deaf ears. Because Sasha wanted to hear absolutely nothing, except that they were being released.

"Maybe," Sasha said, "but John and I had nothing to do with this. We hardly even know you."

"I get that," Helena said. "And I'm sorry you're caught up in this. Hell, I'm sorry I'm caught up in this. And I know that Carolina is not very impressed either. I'm pretty sure her brother right now is pretty pissed off about the whole damn thing too."

"Well, good," Sasha said. "He should be. Whatever he did wrong, he should own up to it and take the punishment."

"Did *wrong?*" Helena asked, her hand immediately going out to stop Carolina. She could feel the vibrating tension in Carolina's frame. "Do you think that her brother did something wrong? And that's why we're here?"

"Of course!" Sasha snapped. "It's only when people do bad things that they get caught up in this shit."

"Like you and me and John and Carolina? Did we do something bad?"

"Of course not!" Sasha said. "Now you're twisting my words."

"Well, I'm not trying to," Helena said, "but Lennox deals in wars, as do these men. And there's no use in blaming anyone. We are on opposite sides here with the kidnappers. We want different things. There's no right or wrong answer when it comes to a war with men on opposite sides. It doesn't necessarily mean either one of them did something that caused harm to the other."

"Is that what you think this is about?" Sasha said with a disbelieving laugh. "He made it very clear that Lennox hurt him and someone else. And that Lennox will pay for the damage he did. And I, for one, agree with him. I think he *should* pay."

"Well then, since your mind is closed on the issue— without any supporting facts, I might add, just the word of a gunman who had us kidnapped—not a whole lot of point in talking to you anymore, is there?" Helena said coolly. "Maybe you can use all those arguments to talk to the kidnappers instead and get yourself out of here." She was getting tired of these two. And fast.

"Sasha stared at her. "Do you think it would work?" she asked cautiously.

"Well, I know John wants to try a similar tactic," Helena said, shaking her head wearily. "So talk to him. You and John figure something out for yourselves."

Helena couldn't really blame the others for wanting to get the hell out of here; it was a tough situation. It was their damn whiny attitudes and blaming posturing that she found fault with. Yes, it was a stressful scene, more so than some of their surgical theaters, set up in war-torn countries, where a stray bomb or bullet could kill them all. Yet that was fate. This was premeditated. This time, if they died here, it was because one of the gunmen had pointed their rifles at them and pulled the trigger.

So, yes. This situation was amped up, even compared to the normal Red Cross scenarios that they found themselves in. Helena just wished that John and Sasha would grow a pair. Where were their humanitarian instincts right now? Obviously those were just for show to impress doctors and to get paid to do a job. Nothing more than that. Helena let out a long sigh.

Despite all she had seen in her life—both at home and on the work fronts—she was still surprised when she found the likes of these cowards, whether dressed up in scrubs or with a mild-manner demeanor. They were all con artists.

Helena wanted John and Sasha to focus on something a little more than themselves, like the bigger picture here. If just for one hour. But Helena knew that was too much to ask for from these wimps. Without a true backbone, people like them fold at the first high winds that blow through. That's just the way they were, inside, regardless of what their outsides looked like.

And Helena wondered. If she were given a choice, would she leave Carolina? She could certainly go and get help and bring people back, but leaving Carolina alone would be a challenging thing to do. She shook her head. No way she could leave Carolina here. Not with the likes of these two left to do … whatever to her best friend in retaliation.

In a different situation, where Carolina was hurt, maybe unconscious, without kidnappers and weak-willed ninnies about, yes. Helena would secure Carolina in the best hiding place she could find and would then race to find help. Something neither John nor Sasha would do for each other, much less for Carolina and Helena.

Just then, John was led back to the cage. He was arguing fiercely with the guard. "I can help you," he said. "I have money."

"It's not about money," the guard said, as he unlocked the door and gave John a hard shove.

"But we don't have anything to do with this!" John said in disbelief. "Why won't you listen?"

The guard stared at him, a hard look on his face. "I listened," he said, "but you said nothing that I care to hear." And he turned and walked away.

John called out, "You don't care that we didn't have anything to do with this?"

The guard shook his head.

"But why? That makes no sense. You say you're doing this because you want her brother? We have nothing to do with her brother or her. You're just creating another bad mess because now our families will be angry too."

The guard turned to look at him. "Do you have any family in the military?"

John frowned and then shook his head. "No."

"Then I don't need to worry," he said and turned and walked out.

Helena wanted to laugh at the look on John's face at the utter disbelief that somebody would be so unreasonable. He didn't get it. She understood there was no getting *it*. There was nothing here to understand. The gunmen didn't care one little bit about who was here and who wasn't here. Well, except for Lennox's absence.

As far as the kidnappers were concerned, it was all about themselves. They had a goal. *Get Lennox. Get payback from Lennox.* The gunmen didn't care who got hurt in the process. It didn't matter that it was a similar attitude to what Lennox would likely have felt when he did whatever *wrong* that they assumed he did. Maybe he'd been so focused on *his* goal that he didn't care about who else got hurt.

But that wasn't anything like the Lennox she knew.

However, John made a good point because the kidnappers *were* creating a new problem. Still none of the kidnappers would care. Because the originating event seemed military-related. So the scarred man had a family member who was hurt by Lennox, someone not in the military? Even with Lennox's secret SEALs ops, no way Lennox would harm a civilian. Of any country. Helena would stake her life on it.

In a way, she already had.

But that wasn't the way most people thought. It was the way of life too many times where nobody cared. And the sooner that John got a handle on that, the better. Helena had learned that lesson the hard way; so had Carolina. They understood that Lennox cared and that there were probably doctors who cared and nurses who cared, but, given the general state of things, nobody else gave a shit.

You were expected to look after your world, look after everything going on in your life, without involving others. And deal with whatever came at you. If you couldn't deal with it, well, shut the hell up and go away. Because nobody gave a shit—that was the bottom line.

Helena groaned slightly and sank back against the cage wall.

"This is your fault," John said, turning on her like a rabid animal.

She opened her eyes to see if he would lunge and attack because that would be a whole different story. "What did I do?" she asked calmly.

"You brought this on us!" he said.

"I'm not so sure about that," she said. "I can see you want to believe it, but that's not logical."

"It is," he swore. "It seriously is."

She shrugged. "Maybe, but this is what we have to deal with. The sooner you accept it, the better."

"There's no accepting this!" he said, shaking his head, almost vibrating in a fury.

"So what do you want to do about it?" she asked, slowly standing up, stepping closer to John. "You want to hit me? Is that what this is all about? Do you need to lash out at Carolina and me to make you feel better? It doesn't matter that we didn't have anything to do with this either. It doesn't matter *to you* that we don't know what's going on and that we have no involvement in whatever happened in the first place."

He looked at her. "How is it possible that you can't know?"

"Because Lennox was in the military—special ops, as a SEAL. Highly covert missions. We don't know anything about his life while he was in the military," she said. "You do realize the secrecy involved in the military, don't you?" She huffed, crossing her arms, a frown on her face.

Seeing John not putting up a fight when first taken by the kidnappers, to turning on her and Carolina so fast, Helena gathered that John had probably failed the physical exam—or the psych test—or maybe never wanted to be in the military in the first place. His ego and his brawn and his brains—more important, his manhood—were again being called into question here, under these adverse conditions.

She knew where he was coming from now. A frightened little boy, putting up the big bully front, hoping she would back down. Wow. Did he ever pick the wrong person for this particular manipulation.

As she continued to assess him, she realized that some of the rigidity had fallen from his back and spine and shoulders and that—maybe, just maybe—it was safe to relax a little bit. "I get that you're upset," she said. "Believe me. None of us are thrilled to be here. None of us *chose* to be here either. But this pseudo-threatening attitude of yours toward Carolina and me won't change anything a damn bit right now."

He snorted and walked to where Sasha was, sitting, staring up at him. He looked at Sasha and said, "Sorry, I tried."

She nodded. "I was trying to figure out what I could do to help. But it's not like the guards want to be reasonable."

"The guards are only focused on what they want," Carolina said. "It doesn't matter what we want."

"So how can we fix that?" Sasha asked. "How can we get them to focus on something else?"

"Well, a diversion would be nice," Helena said, "particularly at the same time when we somehow get the gate unlocked. Maybe then we could escape."

The two of them looked at her. "Do you think so?"

"I don't know for sure," she said. "It's a work in progress right now. Only a theory. What I do know is that, even if we got out of this cage, I'm sure more men with guns are not very far away," she said. "Probably eight of them or even more are right outside this building. So the chances of us breaking out of this place will be harder than we think. So we need to take all that into account as we devise any escape plan."

"I hadn't even figured a way to get out of this cage," Sasha said, slowly climbing to her feet. "So what are you thinking so far?"

"I can probably pick the lock," she said, "but what I don't know is after that."

"And how would you pick the lock?" John whispered, his gaze focused on the gate into the cage.

Helena pulled a bobby pin from her hair and held it up. The two of them frowned at it, looked at the lock, and back at her. She shrugged. "I've done it once or twice before, but I won't know if it'll work here until I try it. Even so, it won't do us any good after that."

"Are you serious?"

"If we try and get caught, it's gonna be worse for us afterward," she said. "Some of us could even get killed in the attempt."

"We have to be strategic," Carolina said. "We have to wait for an opportunity. Then we can get out of here *and* get free and clear. Not just free."

"What'll that take?" Sasha asked, crawling closer.

Helena looked at her. "The arrival of Lennox."

Understanding settled on the other two's faces, and they curled back up in their corner, yet looking a whole lot more relaxed. If nothing else, a rough draft of a plan was in motion. And just having that much gave them a glimmer of hope. Helena wasn't sure that Lennox was even on the way yet. But she did know that, one way or the other, he'd find Carolina. Come hell or high water, Lennox was coming. It was just a matter of when.

LENNOX SHIFTED POSITION. They'd been waiting for hours. His instincts said that something wasn't as it seemed. It was too simple; only one man with a rifle didn't make any sense. The fact that a man with a gun was here at least gave Lennox and Gavin some inclination that maybe they were in the right location, but Lennox couldn't confirm even that much. Which bothered him.

He turned to find his partner. Gavin crept along the fence. There was just enough half-light that their body shapes were merging with whatever was around them. It was a perfect time to skulk. But anybody who was expecting their company would know that too.

Were the prisoners sitting in that one shed? Could they have been locked up in the machine shop? There was a barn too. That was Lennox's first location to search. And the closest building. People often considered a barn only for animals but would keep people penned in there too. But generally farmers needed more accessible ways to get out of a barn than a single door. That observation alone seemed to rule out that his sister was here in Lennox's mind.

Still they had to check out this farm.

Lennox waited for a moment and then moved silently toward the barn. He crouched low along the creek, where lots of brush could camouflage him a bit longer. Then he had a spot of about twenty feet to cross, without any barrier to hide his presence. And, once across, he leaned up against the barn and listened. But he heard nothing, not a creak of old wood nor of an animal shifting.

Lennox spotted a large window close by. He slipped to the side of it and slowly peered inside. But it was impossible to see clearly. And it was not meant to open to let the air inside—or even a curious passerby. Nor was it made for gazing but for simply letting sunshine in. Plus it had dirt caked on it from both sides; not to mention bird poop and dead bugs clung to the outside of it. Even in full sunlight, there was no looking inside through this window.

The door at the end of the barn was half open. Lennox could see that by the way the waning sunlight filtered inside. So he crept softly around the two sides of the barn to get to the other side. Once there, he slid inside, his weapon at the ready, only to find the barn itself was one big empty building. There weren't even stalls in it. No loft. Just four walls and a lot of empty ground for a floor. He glanced around, realizing there was no place for anybody to hide and slid back out the way he'd come. He tapped his ear comm to let Gavin know that this first place on his list was empty.

Next was the shed, but that was technically on Gavin's list of buildings to inspect. And then the large machine shop as well. That was an excellent option in that it was the closest building to the gunman taking his smoke break. But that didn't mean that the shed wasn't a diversion.

Lennox watched Gavin approach the shed, which was big enough for a prison to hold four, and noted a window in the door on the side Lennox could see. Quickly Gavin looked in that window as Lennox watched, and then Gavin switched his position, going to the other side of the shed— and out of Lennox's sight—maybe to look through a window in another door from that side too? Almost immediately Lennox heard the tap on his comm, confirming the captives weren't there.

Damn, that meant the machine shop was their best bet. And was right where that group of four men still loitered inside, plus their smoking gunman right outside hadn't moved, yet had finished his cigarette.

Lennox searched the area, trying to mark a pathway to get closer without being seen by the five guys involved in his next target. No point in taking out the gunman if he didn't have their prisoners. Yet the guy could be one of those happy little target shooters, a jumpy gunman with a quick trigger finger. And, if the smoker engaged with Lennox, somebody would get hurt, and Lennox knew perfectly well it wouldn't be him. So, therefore, he wanted to confirm that the prisoners were here first before any shots were fired.

He wasn't too far from the back end of the machine shop. He waited to listen to the sounds of the world around him. A large truck was going down the road. Using the cover of that noise, Lennox quickly moved from one clump of brush to the other, blending into the background, his shadow merging with the other shadows to keep his presence unknown. He'd been lucky in that he hadn't flushed out any wildlife hiding under the bushes.

As he made his way to the side of the machine shop, he stopped, shifted, and listened. He could hear men on the inside of the building but didn't understand the language. He quickly taped it and ran the clip through a translation app on his cell, inserting an earbud into one ear to get the gist of it. *Farming.* With his phone on Silent, he pocketed it and shifted around the corner ever-so-slightly so that he could take a look. Two men were at forklifts, already holding large pallets. They were dressed in jeans and simple cotton shirts; one was smoking, which wasn't the smartest thing on a job like that, but, hey, people did stupid things all the time.

No sign of prisoners so far but Lennox couldn't see a whole section of the machine shop on the other side of that forklift yet. Somehow he would have to get past this open double door and the four guys inside and go around to the far side, so he could then take a look at what was on that side of the machine. He waited until the men shuffled their positions; then Lennox made his way across the open door and slid down the far wall on the outside. Just as he thought he had safely made it, he heard his comm tap and afterward came Gavin's whispered voice.

"Guard alerted."

"Shit," Lennox whispered under his breath. He couldn't see the guard from where Lennox was, but he could hear that gunman arriving, speaking English, asking if they saw anything. Voices were raised, and one of the other men called out, "Nothing. Nothing here."

The gunman's footsteps seemed to retrace to where he'd been standing before, beside his truck.

Lennox moved carefully, crept up to the window, and took a look at the other half of the machine shop. He found glass and ceramic jugs and what looked like some homemade still.

These guys were probably making moonshine. Without a license in a place like this, they would need somebody on guard. With a rifle.

Even worse, Lennox found no sign of the prisoners. What a huge waste of time.

Swearing, he moved back slightly, sending a message to Gavin that this building appeared to be empty. Or at least not housing his sister and her team. As Lennox walked around the back side of the shop, a man came out a side door and shouted at him. He turned and looked at him and said, "Sorry, in the wrong place."

The man looked at him in confusion, and Lennox realized he didn't understand English. Regardless Lennox's presence would startle the others. He walked up with a big smile on his face, and, when he got close enough, he struck the man hard in the throat, sufficient to disable him and to drop him to the ground.

Racing silently through the encroaching darkness, Lennox made his way back into the bush and then headed to the truck.

There he met Gavin.

"That was close," Gavin said. "They were running illegal whiskey, from what I saw."

"Agreed," Lennox said. "Unfortunately I met up with one guy. He wasn't thrilled, so I put him down."

"You killed him?"

"Hell no. He's down, but he'll remember somebody skulking around his place, and the others will be pissed off at the guard."

"With good reason," he said. "If that were one of our guys, you know that we would have fired him for what we were able to do."

"True enough," Lennox said. "Next target?"

"I'm wondering if that road leading to that farm didn't carry on farther past to another property up in the hills there."

"It's possible the driveway continues on, but it becomes a dirt road. Up on the hill, I was thinking it headed to pastures."

"Maybe, but I don't think we can take that chance. We

need to scope it out for ourselves."

"Shall we drive closer?"

"Could save us a few steps," Gavin added with a shrug.

Lennox had his phone out, GPS running, while he looked at the area maps. "I think we need to go back along this way. Not exactly as far as that, but we would only have a few hundred yards to cross."

That's what they did. Lennox quickly turned the truck around and headed back, following Gavin's instructions. At the new location they parked off to the side of a ditch and crossed over a fence to the designated search area, about seventy-five yards away that led to the other driveway. Passing that as quickly as possible, they realized that this driveway continued for probably half a mile.

They made their way along that road in complete darkness. No vehicles passed by; nothing came by, not even wildlife or a stray dog. When they got to the small rise, they stopped; they found a large settlement below, including a house off to the side of another large machine shed again and what looked like a double-size barn.

"Everybody has multiple outbuildings," Gavin noted.

"Exactly," Lennox said, "but how do we know this is our place? We keep wasting time ruling each one out."

Just then two men came out of the house, both of them strapping rifles over their shoulders.

"Well, that's promising," Lennox said.

One of them called out to another man, and he stood; his form had blended in entirely to the machine shed. But he also had a weapon over his shoulder and a handgun in his right hand.

"Well, that looks even more promising," Lennox said, studying the long machine shed. "That thing's got to be fifty feet long."

"If not more," Gavin said. "I'd say it's at least twenty feet wide. It's that corrugated metal material with likely no windows."

"Which means, only one way in, one way out."

"But likely a second door is in the back," Gavin said, "but it won't be as easy to open or to maneuver through."

"So not a bad prison," Lennox said with a nod. "Far enough away from anyone that, although any gunshots will echo in the hills, nobody will give a shit."

"I think everybody's keeping to themselves out here. They're probably all running something illegal, in one way or another, which keeps them all away from everybody else's business."

"Right," Lennox said. "So how many have we got here? Three in the front right now but how many others do you think are in the house?"

"We can go through the house first."

"Or can use a diversion to flush them out of the house," Lennox suggested.

Gavin considered that and nodded. "How about a fire?" he said, pointing to a large pile of deadwood. "It's small enough not to do too much damage, even if it does take off."

"And, if it takes off, it'll come toward the buildings, and that's what the gunmen will be concerned about."

"Exactly."

"You got a way to start that?"

Gavin grinned, his white teeth flashing in the darkness. "Just wait for it," he said. "You'll have your diversion in no time." And he got up and slipped into the darkness, leaving Lennox all alone.

CHAPTER 7

HELENA MUST HAVE dozed off for a few hours because, when she woke, the building was in complete darkness. Wondering what had woken her—outside of her uncomfortable position, the strange circumstances, and the terror that she'd recently gone through—was something she almost laughed at because she had any number of reasons not to sleep deeply and contentedly. But, when exhaustion had claimed her, she had slept. Maybe not well but she'd take any rest that she could get right now.

Outside she heard footsteps racing and people swearing. She immediately woke Carolina. "Something's happening," she said urgently.

Carolina stared at her, looked around, and then bolted to her feet. "We have to be ready."

"Oh, I agree," Helena said. "Now if only we knew what that would mean."

John mumbled from the far side, "What's the matter?"

"Hear all the shouting and running outside?" she asked him.

He stared at her and slowly sat up. "Do you think it's Lennox?"

"I have no clue," she said.

A man's voice interrupted their conversation. "I hope it is," he said, "because then I'll be ready for him."

That was the scarred man talking. The man in charge. He seemed to leave the building. Another guard slunk out of the darkness. A man she hadn't yet seen before stared at her. "What's going on out there?" she asked.

"Looks like a brushfire."

"Fire?" she cried out, staring at him in shock. "We have to get out of here!"

"I don't give a fuck," he said and spat out what looked like the butt of a cigarette onto the ground.

"A fire will raze this place to the ground," Helena said, waving her arm around at the shed.

"It's metal," he said with a sneer. "It does not burn."

"Maybe not," she said, "but the stuff in it will."

"And how does the fire get in?" he asked, studying her as if she were an ignorant schoolgirl.

"The bales of hay stacked along the back wall would bring it in," she said.

He looked startled for a moment as he turned to study the back wall. He walked past her to the far end of the shed.

Carolina looked at her. "Do you have a plan with that?"

"Maybe," she whispered, "but he has to leave first."

"Why are they always listening to us?" John asked, crawling over to where they were. "It's creepy."

She stood, peering in the darkness, when the door at the far end of the machine shop opened. And the man they'd been speaking with called out something. She saw flames crackling at that end.

"Shit," she said, "that's too damn close." She pulled the bobby pin from her hair, stripped off the plastic coating at one end, and walked over to the lock on the gate. Standing casually, she grabbed the lock and tried to pop it free with the help of her bobby pin.

And, just as she managed it, a voice close to her ear whispered, "Good girl."

She froze, but Lennox took over, taking the lock from her hand, opening the cage, and pulling her free. John woke up Sasha, but Lennox already had Carolina up and out. Lennox led them to the corner of the front doorway and said to Helena, "Race up the hill at that angle," he said, pointing in the right direction. "You're going for that biggest tree as your landmark. Do not make a sound. Just run."

And he got her and Carolina moving as fast as they could. She turned to look behind her to see John and Sasha following. But she had her orders, and she knew one thing— Lennox expected his orders to be obeyed.

And there would be no forgiveness from the kidnappers if Helena and her team didn't get to where they needed to go. She hit the tree and kept on going, not sure where she was supposed to go now. But she saw a vehicle at the far end of a path. She caught sight of an unknown man, and her steps faltered. But he urged her to keep going. She raced up to the truck, eyeing this latest stranger, who whispered, "I'm Gavin. I'm with Lennox. Get in."

Helena hopped into the back seat of the double-cab truck and helped John inside beside her, while Gavin helped Carolina climb into the back seat on the other side of Helena.

As Helena turned to look behind, Lennox picked up Sasha, lagging behind, and carried her as he raced faster and faster. He damn-near tossed Sasha into the back seat of the truck, calling out to Gavin, "Go! Go! Go!"

Gavin hopped into the front of the truck, and, as Sasha was climbing into the back, smashing onto John, Lennox dove into the front seat. Gavin had the vehicle tearing down the road in no time.

Helena wasn't exactly sure where the hell they were going, and she didn't give a damn. She just smiled up at John, who stared at her in shock.

She nodded. "Yes, that's Lennox."

He shook his head, leaned forward, and asked Lennox, "How do you get past everybody?"

Lennox didn't respond.

"A diversion," Helena stated matter-of-factly. "And did you note that not one gunshot went off?" She smiled smugly at John. "That's not what Lennox does. *Unless* he's forced to."

"And how did *you* know?" he blustered, glaring at her, ignoring her barb pointed at him.

"*Diversion?*" she said. "It's simple."

He frowned.

She shrugged. "The only way we could be rescued was if Lennox and his partner had a way to get the gunmen away from us," she said. "So, they started the fire. Then, when our guards left us, that's when I knew it was time to pick the lock."

Lennox twisted to look at her. "Did I teach you that, or did you learn it on your own?"

"You showed me," she said, "and then I learned it on my own."

"Good," he said, "at least you learned something."

She frowned at him. "I've learned a lot."

"Yeah, from me?" He waggled his eyebrows.

She glared at him. "Have you got a plan at this point?"

"Yep, to get the hell away."

"Great," she said. "In other words, no?"

He laughed. "We got this far." Only then something

hard pinged the side of the truck. "Everyone down!"

"Shit!" Gavin growled, and he drove faster.

"I presume we're being followed," she said. She tried to stare out the back of the truck, but bullets shattered the back window.

Lennox immediately ordered them to lie as flat as they could.

And, with all four of them taking up as little space as possible and flush low in the back, they bounced over the rough ground before suddenly hitting a smoother road. The truck picked up speed as it jumped forward.

Helena looked at Carolina. "Well, it's a half-baked idea, but at least it's a plan."

More shots hit the truck but not anybody in the truck.

Carolina grinned. "Trust in Lennox. If anybody can get us out of here, it's him."

Helena didn't need to be told. She already knew that. The only issue was the fact that, right now, they were between a rock and a hard place. Somebody was still firing at them, and she doubted this truck had the gas to keep going the distance. She also didn't think this area was particularly friendly to foreigners.

Just then they hit another rough road and bounced and jostled as the truck tore across new ground. Helena wondered if it even was a road or if they were going across a farmer's field. Crouched down as she was, she couldn't see. She groaned as they hit a particularly rough spot.

"Sorry about the rough road," Lennox said. "We'll be changing vehicles in a few minutes, so get ready."

Immediately she tensed, awaiting his instructions. She hoped they would stop—as in completely—before they were expected to switch vehicles. And suddenly they pulled up somewhere, hit the brakes with great force, and Gavin was out of the truck, opening up one of the rear doors.

Lennox had opened up the other rear door. "Let's go now!" He moved them into an SUV parked at the side. It was older, had no license plates, but would seat six nicely inside. By the time they got into the back seats of the vehicle, it still hadn't started. But Gavin waited while Lennox popped the hood, then did something, and got it fired up. He stepped up into the front passenger seat with his two duffel bags, and they took off across the road again before Lennox got settled.

Helena had no clue where they were and didn't have any idea what direction they were traveling because it was pitch black outside, what with the cloud cover blocking what little moonlight was to be had. Sometimes in the night you saw enough of the shadows to see where you're going—but not tonight. She leaned forward. "How can you guys see where you're going?"

"Gavin is wearing night goggles," Lennox explained. She looked over, and, sure enough, Gavin had some weird glasses over his eyes. "Okay," she said, settling back. "Any idea how to get out of here?"

"We're working on it," he said. "We're in Poland, by the way."

That was a surprise to her. She glanced at the others, who stared back at her wordlessly.

"Anybody got connections in Poland?" Lennox asked.

Everybody shook their heads.

"Sorry, we're no help back here."

"Not an issue," he said. "We're trying to roust up some other means of travel."

"Good," she said. "A flight would be nice. It's the fastest

way out of here. But our IDs, wallets, phones, etc., these guys had it all. I'm not sure what happened to our luggage."

Lennox laughed and picked up his phone to make a call. She wanted to listen in but couldn't hear the conversation anyway. She looked at Carolina, who was huddled up in her seat, quiet, her eyes closed. "Carolina, are you okay?"

"I am," she said. "We're getting out of here. That's all that I care about."

"Well, yes," Helena said, "and no. We're not exactly free and clear yet."

"No," she said, "but my brother is doing what he can. And I have to admit that's usually a whole lot more than anybody else can."

"I get it," John said. "He's some sort of Secret Service spy guy. As long as he gets us out of there, I promise I'll never say a bad word against him again."

"We can't make any guarantees here, not yet," Helena said. "That's not how life works. But he's good, and, if anyone can get us out of this situation, Lennox will."

"I know," John said. "I'd just appreciate no longer being in this mess."

"Exactly," she said, "and hopefully that'll be a distant memory soon."

While they drove through the night, having finally lost their armed pursuers, they pulled into a small town, where they stopped to fuel up. She leaned forward to speak to Lennox, who stood outside her door. "We need food, and we need bathrooms."

"I'll take you," Lennox said. "Nobody is to go on their own."

He opened up the passenger door and let the three women hop out. After that, John hopped out and stood beside Gavin. Lennox led the women to the outdoor washroom with a locked door and that held one person at a time. Sasha went in first. When she came out, Lennox motioned at Helena. She just shook her head and said, "We'll go in together." She opened the door, and she and Carolina walked into the bathroom. They quickly used the facilities, washed, and stepped back out again.

"Coffee and food?" she asked hopefully.

Lennox looked at her in the half-light, studying her face, and then his sister's. "Are you two okay?"

Carolina smiled, nodded, and said, "We're fine. I took one hit. So did Helena."

He swore when he realized that his sister had been smacked. He studied her face in the light of the bathroom and asked, "How bad?"

She reached up, cupped his face on either side, and said, "I'm fine, Lennox."

"Good thing," he growled, and he hauled her into his arms and gave her a big hug.

Helena stood off to the side, jealous in a way because she'd been looking for that human contact, which she had yet to get. Although she had known Lennox over many, many years, still he didn't know a lot about her. Like her feelings for him. And the heat that flashed inside her every time she saw him. And yet he'd scared her back then, with that kiss, and she'd turned away from that confusion—that heat—and had promptly found someone the exact opposite of Lennox.

While she stood here, looking out at the SUV, an arm reached out and snagged her, as Lennox hauled her in for his hug with his sister. She burrowed her face tight against him, hating that trembling coming from inside her.

But, once again, Lennox had come through.

That's the one thing—Carolina could always count on her brother. Hell, Helena didn't remember anyone having her back. She'd been walking alone for all her life, whereas Carolina always had her brother there to help. He let her make the decisions and the choices in her life and let her fall when they were terrible choices, but he'd always been there to give her a hand when she needed it. Helena had Carolina, but she hadn't had Lennox. Helena wondered just how different that would have made her world?

Right now it was huge. She was damn grateful for the warm arms that held her close.

When he finally released them, he said, "Get back into the SUV. I'll see if any food's available to go with that coffee."

She nodded. "That would be good."

"Do you all drink coffee?"

Carolina flashed a smile at him. "Of course we do," she said, "but I think two of them take sugar."

"I'll get it," he said. They raced back to the SUV and hopped into the back seat. This vehicle had three rows of seats, and they were in the middle; John and Sasha sat in the back. John leaned forward and asked, "Is he getting something from inside?"

"Depends if there is anything to get," Helena said. "I said we could all use some coffee and food, if that was an option."

"Yes," Sasha said, "both of those would be lovely."

"Safety would be our priority though." They sat quietly in the vehicle, but her heart pounded as she studied to see if they were still being followed. She leaned forward and said, "Hi, Gavin. My name is Helena. I'm a friend of Carolina's."

Gavin tossed her a quick grin. "I've heard about you," he said. "Lennox doesn't talk much, but he has mentioned you."

"All good things I hope," she quipped, but she was pretty damn sure it wasn't.

He just shrugged and didn't say anything.

As she watched the store, Lennox walked out of the small gas station, carrying a tray with four coffees. He walked to the passenger side. She rolled down her window and accepted all four. "Are you getting any for yourself and Gavin?"

He nodded. "I'll be right back." And he headed back inside.

Helena handed out the coffees. She smiled at Gavin. "He will get you one too, won't he?"

"He will," Gavin said, and she realized that they must know each other pretty well. "Our kidnappers said it was a revenge for Lennox. That they wanted Lennox to pay for a betrayal."

Gavin spun in his seat and looked at her. "Can you explain what he said exactly?" And then he stopped her. "Hang on. Let's wait until Lennox gets back."

Just then the store's door opened again, Lennox pushing it with his shoulder and then his foot, as he stepped out carrying another tray of coffee and a large bag. He handed the tray through the open window to Gavin and then walked around the front to his side and hopped inside. Gavin removed the two coffees from the tray, placing them in cup holders, and said, "Helena has something to say."

She quickly explained what the scarred man had said about it being a betrayal.

Gavin just looked at Lennox, and Lennox looked back.

He shook his head. "Can you describe him?"

"He's got a bad scar on his cheek," Carolina said. "And it's deep. It would have involved some jaw surgery likely, and he's got a burn mark on his neck."

"The burn goes down the inside of his shirt," Helena added. "And I would have called it third-degree burns. We saw a lot of scar tissue, and it looks like layers of it."

"I agree with that too," Carolina stated. "His muscle damage was quite extensive around the neck, where his longer hair covers part of it but does not go up as high as the jaw."

"What about the rest of him?"

John supplied that info. "Six-foot, 205 pounds, light brown hair, short with a light wave. His eyes are dark, maybe brown. Fair skin as if maybe European descent."

"Dress?"

"Fatigues," Sasha added. "No hats among the kidnappers, no gloves among them, and I would have said military work boots."

"Combat boots?"

"Yes," Sasha said.

"Weapons?" Gavin started up the engine and put the SUV back on the road while they talked.

Nobody had any details on the weapons, outside of the fact that they were carrying rifles or machine guns, plus handguns. "Outside of the original kidnapping crew, once we landed in that cage in Poland, we saw three different men who stood guard on a rotating basis," Helena added.

"We saw six," Lennox added. "All six will be after us."

"It was very personal," John said from the back row. "We tried to explain that we had nothing to do with it, and he didn't care."

"Of course not," Lennox said. "You were just part of the bait. Once they started shooting prisoners, it ups the ante as to when they'd get around to shooting my sister."

John stared at him and then collapsed back. "I was afraid you were gonna say something like that."

"Sorry," Lennox said, "but you were caught at the wrong place at the wrong time."

"All four of us were in the wrong place at the wrong time." Helena continued, "We all caught the same lift to the airport, so we were dropped off at the same time. Two of us were heading to Munich, and the other two were heading somewhere else, but all were international destinations. It's almost as if the kidnappers were waiting for us. We were led to another vehicle and tossed into the back."

"They approached you at the airport?"

"Yes, we were quickly surrounded by four men in military fatigues, who had handguns," Helena supplied, as she dredged up the memory of when they were first picked up and moved into a vehicle. "They didn't say much. But they didn't need to. The weapons are a universal language." Then she settled back with her coffee.

Lennox opened the bag he'd brought with him and handed out sandwiches and pepperoni sticks and string cheese and bags of chips. She gratefully accepted everything coming her way, making sure that it was an even breakdown, but Lennox had bought everything times six. She ate her sandwich first, then both the cheese and the pepperoni. As she looked at Carolina, she was not eating her lunch. "You're not hungry?"

Carolina shook her head. "My stomach is still not so great."

"You need to eat," Lennox said.

"I know. *I need to keep up my energy just in case we need to run again,*" she said in a comical voice. "But since my head injury, my stomach has been on the queasy side."

"Not a whole lot we can do about that here and now," Helena said. "I'm pretty sure you had a slight concussion."

"Most likely," she said. "And it doesn't matter now because I'm healing. That's what counts."

"True enough," she said. "It's all good."

Lennox shot Helena a questioning look, one eyebrow raised. She nodded. "She'll be fine."

He settled back.

"So you listen to Helena now, huh?" Carolina asked, her tone sharp. "Without listening to me?"

"Yes," Lennox said, "because you've been known to not tell me the whole truth every once in a while."

"Seriously?" she said in outrage.

"Yes," he said, "if it suits you."

"That's just being a sibling," Carolina said with a laugh. "And having you as an older brother wasn't easy either."

"I've been there every time you needed me."

"You've been there every time I've needed you and more," Carolina said guiltily. "I did tell you how much I love you, right?"

He let out a bark of laughter. "Many times and often as you were ready to hit me."

She grinned. "Again that's siblings."

The wrangling continued back and forth, and it helped to ease the atmosphere in the vehicle.

At a pause in the conversation, Sasha spoke suddenly from the back row of seats. "Do you think we're out of danger?"

Lennox turned to look at her and shook his head. "No,

we are not. Not until we can get you out of this country. Yet ... considering you were tracked from Africa, kidnapped in Germany, then taken to Poland, I'm not sure that that's even the correct answer here."

Sasha stared at him. Her eyes were a vast well of fear. "But John and I should be safe once we're back in the US, right?"

Lennox considered that, shrugged, and said, "*Potentially*, yes."

"*Potentially?*" she questioned him, her voice turning ominous. "What do you mean by that?"

He glanced at Gavin, and Gavin glanced back at him.

"What does that silent glance mean?" John interrupted.

"The problem is," Lennox said, "we have to put a stop to this."

"Sure, I get that," Sasha said, "but why is it that we won't be out of danger even if we're back home again?"

"You will be safe once we capture the guy behind this," he said, "but otherwise you are in danger of always being able to identify him."

The other two sat back slowly and stared. "And that'll be a problem?"

"Depends on how he feels about it," Lennox said. "I don't understand who this guy is, or why he feels he has a grudge against me, but, as long as he's holding that grudge, then obviously my sister and her best friend will be in more danger than the two of you. However, if he's considering his actions from a criminal level and the chances of being charged with a crime, then to not be identified will be important to him. Therefore, they'll want to keep you from identifying him."

"And that doesn't sound very good either," Sasha said

faintly, "because that sounds like he'd planned on killing us."

"I would suspect so," Helena said quietly. "The fact that he didn't hide his face right from the beginning is very indicative of his intentions."

"And that seriously sucks."

"Obviously but that doesn't change the facts right now," Lennox added.

"So, you'll go after this guy?" Sasha asked.

"Right?" John repeated.

Everybody looked at Lennox.

Without hesitation he gave a crisp nod and said, "Yes. I'm going after this guy because he went after my sister."

LENNOX KNEW THEY needed to hear that, but they wouldn't like knowing that it wouldn't be so cut-and-dried in reality. The mastermind behind the kidnapping had skills, money, freedom to move as he needed to, and he had the know-how to hunt down people who were close to Lennox. He looked at his sister. "It might be time for an extended holiday."

She wrinkled up her face. "Well, I was looking for a short one. I'm not sure about an extended one."

"*Extended*," Gavin said in a hard voice. "All of you should consider it."

"Well, I just handed in my notice," Sasha said. "That's exactly what I was planning."

Helena looked at her. "I didn't know that," she said. "Are you done, or did you just give your vacation notice?"

"I'm done," she said. "They owed me time off anyway. So I just took it as part of my leave."

"Wow," Helena said, sinking back in the seat, thinking

about that. "We did get several more doctors in, so, in theory, they could do without us for a while."

"They could," Carolina said, "but you know how we feel about that."

"Sure, but we can't get in the way of Lennox going after this guy."

"And how would going back to work put us in Lennox's way?" John asked.

"This guy is determined to make Lennox pay, and so the scarred guy will come after us, no matter where we are," Helena said. She tilted her head as she stared at Lennox and asked, "Why don't you use us as bait?"

John snorted. "That's the most reasonable suggestion I've heard yet. As long as you keep me out of it."

"Me too," Sasha snapped.

Helena shot them both a hard look. "That's just because you'd like to see us pay for you being involved. You blame us."

Lennox turned, his steady gaze on John.

John shifted uncomfortably. "Okay, so maybe we were a little harsh in our assessment of the scenario."

"Don't go blaming Carolina and Helena for this," Lennox said. "Sounds like this guy wants me to pay for something. Yet I don't know this guy. Yes, it's an ugly scenario, and it is what it is. But you can't go blaming each other. And we can't have you guys being the bait." Now Lennox stared down Helena.

"Not me," Sasha said. "They're the ones who count. John and I want to go home."

Lennox nodded slowly. "I get that, and we're doing our best to get you home. As for my sister and Helena, well, if he went to this much effort, I can't imagine that he's gonna walk away at this point."

"No, he probably isn't," Sasha agreed. "So we need to get the hell out of here."

"We'll be on our way back to Warsaw pretty quickly," Gavin said.

"And how close is *pretty quickly?*" John asked.

Just then Gavin pulled into a supermarket parking lot, but everything was closed for the night. Big streetlamps were on the side, but a massive green space was in the center, and he pulled off under the lights, turned toward the back seats, and waited. "Finish your coffees," he said.

Helena looked at her coffee, tossed back the rest of it, and returned all the garbage to Lennox, who was collecting everything. He made one trip to a trash can sitting off to the side, came back, removed his duffel bags, looked at Carolina, and asked, "Are you ready?"

She groaned. "I might as well be," she said, "because, with you, it's now or never."

In the distance, they heard a helicopter. He smiled at them and said, "Our ride is here."

"Oh, awesome," Sasha said. They hopped out and walked over to him. "Can it take us wherever we need to go?"

"No, it's taking us into Warsaw," he said. "We'll catch flights out later tomorrow."

"Any chance of a shower and a real nap first?" John asked. "We've been traveling forever."

"At the hotel, yes. We can't get flights out before noon tomorrow anyway."

With the helicopter coming in and sending dust and dirt flying everywhere, he quickly led them to the chopper and helped them up into the back seats. With the duffel bags stowed in the helo, the vehicle was left behind, and they were lifted into the air. Lennox glanced around to make sure everybody was buckled in place. He caught Helena's eye.

She smiled at him. "Thank you."

When he looked at her, that same damn jolt hit him in the heart every time. He gave a clipped nod. "You're welcome."

"Well, you don't have to make it sound like the only reason I'm being rescued is that I'm with Carolina," she said.

He winced inside; they always bounced off each other, both of them trying to ignore their feelings, but, at the same time, making any communication harsher as they tried to avoid saying what needed to be said.

"It isn't that," he said. "Let's get to Warsaw, and we can get something arranged to get you guys out of there."

She nodded. "But it's not like the helicopter ride is a big secret."

"I'm counting on it," he said quietly. Helena looked at him in surprise, but he gave her a half smile. "Much better to bring them to us than to play in their backyard."

"Oh," she said in surprise.

Lennox shrugged. "Remember? It's what we do."

CHAPTER 8

THE HELICOPTER LANDED on a hotel roof. They were quickly led down to their assigned rooms. Two suites. Helena thought that the women would be in one and that the men would be in the other. Instead Gavin was with John and Sasha in one, and Lennox was with her and Carolina in another. That made just as much sense when she thought about it because, in no way, would Lennox leave his sister alone.

As they walked in, Helena saw two bedrooms and a small sitting room. "We didn't need anything so fancy," she said.

"We have a connecting door regardless," he said, as he walked over and rapped hard.

The door opened immediately, and there was Gavin.

Lennox said, "Let's leave the door open."

"Got it," Gavin said.

In the background, Helena could hear the other two, discussing rooms, and then John saying that he would shower first. Helena looked at Carolina. "What about you?"

Carolina gave her half a stare. "What about me?"

"Bed or shower?"

She looked at the bathroom and then at the bed and said, "Tough to call. Maybe I'll have a quick shower, if you don't mind."

"Sure. Go have yours now," Helena said. She walked to the couch in the sitting area, plunked herself down, and said, "Was there any food left?"

"Here," Carolina said, and she turned and tossed the sandwich she still held in her hand.

"Aren't you gonna need it later?"

"We're in town now. We can get more food," Lennox said. "If you're hungry, eat."

"Thanks." She quickly opened up the sandwich and ate it slowly, as she waited for Carolina to get out of the shower. She watched as Lennox dug in one of his duffel bags, brought out a laptop, set it up on the small table here, and started sending messages. "Are those emails?"

He shook his head. "No, it's my team."

"Oh," she brightened at that. "Glad to know you have a team."

He looked at her with a puzzled look on his face.

Self-consciously, she shrugged. "Well, it's better than having to work alone."

"Well, there's always Gavin," he said, pointing out the obvious.

"I know," she said. "Just ignore me."

He shot her another strange look and went back to his laptop.

She always felt uncomfortable and awkward around him. There was just so much possibility between them, and yet so much that was wrong. Such was her life.

She finished the sandwich and hopped up, walked over to the kitchenette, and popped the wrapper in the garbage. There she grabbed some water from the tap. She had no idea if it was good to drink or not. She tasted it hesitantly, and, although it had an odd taste, it probably wouldn't kill her, so she had a bigger drink. She leaned back against the sink, just thankful to be here.

Carolina opened the bathroom door and said, "I'm done, and I'll be in bed." She walked out with a towel on her head and a robe on, heading to the bedroom she'd chosen. She entered and closed the door.

Although their suite had two bedrooms, it didn't leave one for Lennox. "Are you gonna sleep?" Helena asked him.

"Part of the time," he said. "I'll be doing shifts with Gavin. That's why we're keeping the connecting door open, so we can hear from both sides."

"Where are you gonna sleep?" she asked, staring at him. She chewed on her bottom lip. He deserved a good night's sleep more than she did. He'd gone through all the problems of tracking them down. She felt guilty as hell taking the only other bed. "I can sleep with your sister."

"Don't worry about it," he said. "I'm fine on the couch."

She looked at the couch, then looked at him. "It might be long enough," she said, "but no way that couch will hold your girth."

At her worry, he looked at her in surprise. "You're saying I'm fat?"

"Like hell," she said, "but you're big."

He shrugged. "I'll be fine. Don't worry about it. Go and grab a shower."

Helena sighed. "Okay, but remember I offered."

"Point taken," he said with a clipped nod. "Now go have your damn shower, please."

She walked into the bathroom, slammed the door with a little more force than necessary, and stripped down. Only now, as she stood here completely nude, did she realize she had no other clothes. What had happened to their luggage?

She'd had only the one carry-on bag and her purse. Was her carry-on back where they'd been kept prisoner? She wanted it, but there was no going back now. … Could Lennox get it somehow?

Swearing, she hopped under the hot shower and shampooed her hair and scrubbed herself from top to bottom. All the time, her mind raced, figuring out just what she was supposed to do. She remembered getting out of the airport shuttle when they had arrived at the Munich airport, and a porter having taken their luggage. Was there any chance it was still sitting at the airport? Maybe the kidnappers only had their purses, phones, and wallets?

She quickly dried off, wrapped up in a towel, realizing that Carolina had grabbed a robe, but no more were here. Maybe another was in the second bedroom, but, of course, Helena hadn't looked for one there.

First, she scooped up her clothing—dirty, dusty, and not what she wanted to put back on again—and realized she would have to put on her underwear regardless. Quickly redressed in panties and a bra, then wrapped back up again with the towel, she grabbed the rest of her dirty clothes, walked out to her bedroom, where she looked for a robe, but there wasn't one. Of course not. She dropped her clothes on the bedroom floor and headed out to ask Lennox, "What happened to our luggage?"

He looked up at her. "It was picked up at the airport. The porter took it inside, but, when you guys didn't reappear, he contacted security."

"Any chance of getting it?"

"It's on its way to the airport, now that we have a location for you," he said. "With any luck, we should get it here in the morning."

"Fresh clothing would be nice," she said. "We all need our passports too, but the kidnappers had them."

He didn't even look up and nodded. "We're working on it."

"Thank you," she said, and then, as she walked back to the bedroom door, she added, "Have a good night."

And again he didn't look up.

Pissed for some reason, more because he looked like he was ignoring her, she said, "That's if you're even listening to me."

Exasperated, he gave a heavy sigh, turned, looked at her, and said, "Good night." And then he spun back around again.

She walked into her room and closed the door and threw herself on the bed. She had no reason to be upset at him. But it was so very typical of every time they'd met. At least since they had kissed. Now everything sounded harsh and just bounced off each other. But she was tired, worn out, and didn't want to wear a bra to bed. She took it off, dropped it to the floor in her pile of clothing, and crawled into the bed, in just her panties. Realizing that she was safe, and they were back in the city, and chances were that she'd be home again pretty damn soon, she rolled over and fell asleep.

IT'S ALMOST AS if Lennox could hear the moment that Helena had relaxed enough to fall asleep. He knew what was wrong between them, but no way was she ready to deal with the issue. Yet it had always been there between them. He'd struggled to not turn around and to see her rosy from a shower, wrapped in a towel. His blood pressure always rose whenever he was around her. Still she'd finally gotten the message and gone to her room. He needed a couple days with her to figure out if this was something they wanted to pursue or if they could walk away from it. But that needed time together, and that was something they avoided at all costs. Which was too damn bad.

Maybe now they'd be forced to address the issue, one way or the other.

Gavin walked through the adjoining rooms and asked, "You okay to stay up for the first watch?"

Lennox nodded. "You did most of the driving. Go rest," he said. "I'll see you in four hours."

With that, Gavin turned and headed back into his suite. Lennox was waiting for Keane to come back on the chat box. When he did, Lennox asked him, **Any news on the search of the identifying marks? How about pictures to match my enemy list?**

I'm sending a series of photos, he typed, **posting them via this link.**

When the link came up, Lennox studied the faces and saw the first man with deep facial scars and neck burns. He recognized a couple guys with similar wounds, but Lennox didn't have any reason to think those guys were after him. Hearing an odd sound, he turned to see his sister, standing at the doorway to her bedroom, her robe back on.

She looked at him. "I was coming for water," she said, as she padded quietly toward him. "You're trying to find the kidnapper?"

Lennox took the opportunity to pull out a chair for her and said, "If you've got a moment, do you want to take a look through these photos?"

She scrolled through the faces, one after each other.

"How come so many men have disfiguring marks like this?" she asked in amazement.

"War is a bitch," Lennox said, "and the injuries are very unforgiving."

She kept going and said, "I don't recognize anybody here." She clicked through three more and then a fourth and a fifth and stopped. Lennox looked at the one she'd stopped at, but she clicked back, and she said, "That's him. ... At least I think it's him," She hesitated, then pulled back slightly to view the face from an angle.

"What makes you think it is him?"

"The scar in that cheek," she said, "it was profound. As in deep into the actual cheek itself."

He studied the scar and nodded. "And some marks are on his neck, but they are hard to identify." He asked her, "What about the nose, the hair?"

"Well, his hair is long now," she said, "compared to the buzz cut in that photo." She looked at it and nodded. "Confirm with Helena," she said, "but I would say that's him."

"Did you recognize any other kidnappers in here?"

"No," she said. "I would recognize the guy who looked after us most of the time," she said, "but this scarred one was the guy who wanted you, and he is also just so very identifiable because of his scars."

"Right," he said. "Now get your water and go back to bed."

She beamed, reached up, kissed him on the cheek, and said, "You really should just go to her. You know that, right?" She walked over and grabbed her water, leaving him gaping at her, his mouth open.

"You didn't just say that," he said.

She stood at the kitchenette, drank her water, put the glass on the counter, turned to look at him, and smiled. "If you guys are staying apart because of me," she said, "that's the worst reason yet."

He shoved his hands in his pockets and leaned back into his chair. "More because of Helena's last relationship."

"That would make more sense," she said with a nod. "But still no reason to avoid a relationship because of that."

"She went through what you went through."

"She did," Carolina acknowledged. "That doesn't mean she's broken."

"Are you broken?" He zeroed in on that one statement.

She sighed. "No, I'm not. I'm just now very wary."

"And she isn't?"

"She is, true," Carolina said quietly. "But you were before that marriage, and you are after that marriage. You're constant. She's not afraid of you."

He frowned at that. "It's still a bad idea," he announced.

"Maybe," she said with a chuckle. "But it should be fun while you guys are at it. Besides, it would be a lot easier on the rest of us if you guys got it out of your system."

"That's just sex you are talking about there," he said.

"Glad you recognize that," she said but smiled, walking toward him. "And, if that's what she wants, then go for it. But the thing is, it's *not* what you want. Otherwise, you would have engaged a long time ago with Helena in a one-night stand or whatever *or* would have just moved on. Yet it hasn't left you alone. *She* hasn't left you alone in all these years because it's got nothing to do with sex. Sure, sex is a great enhancer. It's bonding. It's a great way to come together and to enjoy each other," she said, "but there's so much more between you."

"No," he said, his voice harsh. "There can't be."

That wording—and his stark tone—stopped Carolina in her tracks. "And why is that?"

He struggled to come up with an answer but couldn't seem to formulate one.

"Like I said," Carolina said in a warning voice, "I'm not just your little sister anymore. I still need help at times," she said, "but nobody could have foreseen this scenario. And so, if you're thinking that you're avoiding her because of me, because you don't want to disrupt her relationship with me or the relationship between the two of us as brother and sister," she said, "that's just wrong."

"Maybe," he said. "But what if something goes wrong? I don't want to do anything to upset you."

"I don't think that'll happen," she said. "We've weathered some pretty rough times."

"And I'm not sure she's ready."

"You mean, you're not sure *you* are ready?" she said.

"It's dangerous," he admitted. "Look what happened to you—and Helena—with the kidnapping, and that's just because you're my sister."

"Not necessarily," she said. "This is, like I said, a bizarre scenario."

"True." He nodded. "But it happened. So we don't want it to keep happening. I don't want to get close to Helena and then have people coming after her because she's important to me."

"Really?" Carolina asked with a smile. "How are you gonna stop that?"

He frowned and stared off in the distance.

"Because you realize it's *already* happened. Sure they came after me because I'm your sister. But I'm pretty darn sure that the kidnappers know how close you two are already."

"They can't know," he said, "because I don't even know what I am to Helena."

"Maybe not," she said. "However, you already know how important she is to you. You just hope nobody else does."

"*Does* anybody else?" His voice sounded harsh to him as well.

She smiled. "You mean, does *she* know?"

He hesitated and then gave a nod.

Carolina smiled again, bigger this time, shook her head, and said, "No, I don't think so."

Immediately he let out a sigh of relief.

"But I don't think that's a good thing," Carolina said. "Something's between the two of you, and I think you're cheating yourselves if you don't acknowledge it and at least see what is there."

"*Cheating ourselves?*" he said with a smile. "I'm not so sure about that."

"You won't know unless you try," she said, "and, as we have found out yet again, life is fleeting. It can end in a heartbeat, usually when you least expect it."

"Are you ever gonna have another relationship?" he asked her.

"I will," she said, "when I find a man who doesn't scare the crap out of me."

Instantly his face thinned with anger.

Carolina shook her head. "No," she said. "That's the wrong wording. I'm not afraid of men. I'm afraid of my judgment. And I can tell you that that's a big part of Helena's problem too. We thought we knew what we were doing. We thought we trusted the men we had chosen, but the fact of the matter remains that we made crappy decisions. That's what's stopping her. That's what's stopping me. What we don't want is for that to stop you too."

CHAPTER 9

HELENA HEARD PART of the conversation as she lay curled up in bed. The voices woke her from an uneasy sleep. She'd hoped for a deeply relaxing and rejuvenating sleep instead of the sounds of her best friend's conversation with her brother drifting toward her. It was interesting to hear Carolina's take on Helena's own abuse experience and Lennox's replies. Helena realized just how screwed up they all would be when going into future relationships.

With their backgrounds as victims of abuse, the worst that any relationship could offer, both women were hesitant to move forward. Helena knew that Lennox had absolutely none of the same qualities of her ex-husband; maybe that's why he'd been her ex? Lennox was also a very fit and powerful man, and, if he ever did turn ugly, Helena wouldn't have a hope in hell. It was hard to take a chance, hard to take that step forward. In her heart she trusted him, but did her mind? … Moody, she lay in bed, wondering what her options were.

First off, they had to get home safe and sound, and next, well, she'd look at that when the time came. She let herself drift off to sleep again, waking several more times throughout the night, tossing and turning. When she finally did wake up in the morning, Carolina walked in with a smile on her face.

Helena yawned and asked, "What time is it?"

"It's ten a.m.," she said. "You slept late."

"No," she said, "I just finally got to sleep around four. It was terrible before that, and I'm still so tired."

"I'm sorry you didn't sleep well," Carolina said. "I'm only waking you up," she said, "because food has been ordered. It will be here soon."

"Perfect," Helena said, around a second yawn. "Did our luggage arrive?" She sat up in bed, looking around for her carry-on bag.

"They're due in the next five to ten minutes. Not sure about our purses."

She frowned. "Well, I don't want to go out there not dressed, and I don't want to redress in my dirty clothes if I have fresh ones coming," she said, "so how about I just stay here?"

"Coffee is out there though," Carolina said with a coaxing smile.

"Any chance of a room delivery?" Helena asked hopefully.

Carolina laughed. "I'll see." She disappeared from the room.

Helena smiled. That was the thing about good friends. You could ask them to go the distance, and one little step farther, if it was something you wanted. When the door opened again though, Lennox stepped in. He held a cup of coffee in his hand. "The luggage just arrived downstairs," he said. "We'll have it up here for you in a few minutes."

She beamed. "Thank you. I love the prompt service with our clothes. Any news on our purses and IDs?"

"Yep. We've got them too. Two of our men came in behind us and cleaned out any sign you were ever there."

"Perfect." She felt such a relief to know they could go home now with their proper identification in hand. She held up her cup. "Thanks for the coffee."

"Well, you won't get room delivery all the time," he said with a grin. His gaze lingered, and Helena realized that, since she'd gone to bed with just panties on, an awful lot of skin probably showed. She tugged the sheet a little bit higher and gave him a good frown.

"What's that look for?" he asked.

"Because of the one on your face."

"I like what I see," he said. "You can hardly blame a guy for that."

"I don't blame you," she said. "I just know that we're in this silent truce to stay physically away from each other."

"Maybe that's the wrong thing," he said, standing there with his hands on his hips as he studied her.

"And what brought that on?" she asked, straightening in surprise, trying to mask the shock to her system. As his words mirrored her own internal conversation, she didn't know what to say. *This was about his conversation with Carolina last night.* "It's been what, five years?"

"Right," he said, "five years, and we're both five years older."

"Maybe," she said, "but maybe I'm not any wiser."

"I don't know about that," he said. "I think you've been through enough that you've probably learned a lot."

"I have," she said, as she shuffled up against the headboard, uncomfortably keeping her sheet up high. She waved him toward the door. "It's not a good idea."

"Well, maybe I've changed my mind," he said in a challenging voice, his fingers spreading on his hips as he rocked on his heels slightly. "I've had five years to think about it."

"So have I," she said, hating the bitterness in her voice. "I'm not the same person anymore."

"You can't hide away forever."

She narrowed her gaze at him. "I don't plan on it," she said. "I'm not carrying a grudge against men, if that's what you're thinking—or afraid of them. I got myself into a shitty situation. But that doesn't mean I want to get into another relationship right now."

"I admire the fact that you did get yourself out of that one," he said. "I can't imagine that the two of you were very comfortable in your marriages."

"No," she said, "I wasn't, and, therefore, I won't be too eager to jump back into something like that."

"Well, you shouldn't jump back into *anything* like that," he said, "but you also know that I'm not like that."

She frowned up at him again. "Where is this coming from?"

He shrugged. "Maybe I've been thinking."

Her eyebrows rose. "About me?" She wasn't sure what to think about that. They had had one hell of a fiery kiss and, by mutual agreement, had backed off, deciding it was not smart to move forward. As a way to forget him, she'd gone in the opposite direction. Only it didn't work. She'd always cared. So why was she still arguing, when it's what she wanted? "Nothing has changed. Your sister is still between us."

"Yeah, and I wonder why we put her there?" he said quietly. "You and I both love her. That won't change whether we're together or not."

"Well, considering we're not together," she said, "we don't know that."

"I'm not explaining this very well," he said, his gaze first on her, then her coffee. "We'll pick it up later. Drink your coffee. The luggage should be here soon." And he pivoted and walked out.

She sat here, stunned, sipping her coffee, realizing that the conversation last night between sister and brother had potentially gone a lot deeper than the tidbits she'd heard. She would have to ask Carolina about that.

Just then Carolina walked in with her purse and Helena's purse. "We got them," she said. She dropped Helena's on her lap and then sat down at the end of the bed and said, "Mine appears to be intact. I've got my money, my passport, all my cards even."

"Wouldn't that be lovely?" Helena exclaimed. She checked out her purse and nodded. "It looks like everything's here." At the bottom of her purse was a large-tooth comb; she snatched it and grinned. "How I missed the simple things in life." She quickly combed her hair, plaited it in the back, and curled the braid around her shoulder.

"You look about twelve years old now," Carolina said.

"You're the one who looks twelve," she said teasingly. "I'm at least fourteen."

The two women laughed, both of them welcoming the lighter atmosphere and the chance to release some of the stress from the last few days.

"Oh, our suitcases are here too." Carolina hopped up. "I'll go grab yours." And she dashed out again.

Helena smiled, overjoyed to have her belongings back. There was just such a sense of loss, panic almost, when she didn't have her IDs or a credit card or any cash on hand. It was one thing to be at an airport, where there were assistants and phones and bank machines. And people to contact for help. But, when you were caught in the middle of nowhere,

where you didn't even know the language, … it made you vulnerable.

Carolina returned with Helena's single carry-on bag. "Lennox said we can't use our phones yet, in case the kidnappers are tracking us that way. He'll let us know when it's okay later. I'll go get changed," she said.

She dropped Helena's luggage on the floor for her and disappeared again, closing the door behind her. Helena finished her coffee, put it down, then stood and brought her bag onto the bed and opened it. There she took out leggings and a T-shirt and clean underwear. Dressed and feeling a whole lot better, she rolled up her dirty clothes, put them in a travel-size laundry bag, and stuffed them into the back of her carry-on. She hoped she'd be home pretty soon, but, if it wasn't to be, then she could always rinse these out somewhere. And, with that, she picked up the empty coffee cup and headed out to the main room.

With perfect timing, the doorbell rang. She looked over to see Gavin already at the door, opening up for a trolley, followed by a second one.

"Wow, you ordered some serious food," she said with a happy cry.

"Some serious appetites are here," Lennox said. "Not to worry. You won't starve."

"Didn't expect to," she said with a grin. And, sure enough, as she looked at her options, she found a stack of pancakes, toast, scrambled eggs, some fruit, and little individual yogurts for each of them. She sat down with the rest of the crew and reached for a small yogurt and a spoon first.

"Make sure you eat more than that," Lennox said.

"I will," she promised. But she sat back with the yogurt

and ate it slowly, enjoying the slide of the tangy, creamy texture down her throat. With that gone and everybody else digging into the pancakes, she got her plate and filled it.

Carolina, seated at her side, had already eaten through her pancakes and eggs and was now working on toast. Helena looked at her best friend and said, "You must be feeling better. And starving."

"I am, on both accounts," Carolina said. "You don't know when the next meal will pop up."

"I hope there'll be regular meals from now on," Sasha said bluntly, "because I don't ever want to go through this again."

"I hear you," John said, "but it is a lesson. I find myself on Carolina's train of thought that we need to eat because we can."

"There will be more food," Gavin reassured them.

"Promise?" Helena asked. "Because, otherwise, you know not a scrap of food will be left here."

"Good," Lennox said. "No need for any to remain. Because we paid for it, we might as well eat it. And we can't take it with us."

"Good point," Helena said and took another bite. By the time she was done though, she was overdone. She should have stopped halfway through, but her eyes have been much more concerned about making sure she ate. She wondered how long it took being a captive before that mind-set became permanent. She would already have to watch this urge to eat everything in sight; otherwise she'd end up gaining a ton of weight. And it wasn't necessary. Not for feeding her body.

It was a security thing, an internal panic that she would starve. But she knew she was a long way from that. When she finally put down her fork and pushed back her plate, she groaned and said, "Outside of a cup of coffee, I'm stuffed."

"We'll get another pot of coffee," Gavin said. "We'll just empty these trolleys and take them back out again."

Everybody got up to organize the dishes on the trolleys. Helena went in the opposite direction to grab her coffee cup to keep it with her and returned to the couch, where she curled up into a corner. Her laptop had been in her carry-on bag and was still there, for which she was also damn grateful. She grabbed it and sat down again.

"What are you doing with that?" Lennox asked.

"I wanted to send a couple messages."

He looked up, frowned, and then shook his head. "No," he said, "no communication."

She glared at him. "Seriously?"

"Yes, seriously," he said. "We don't want the kidnapper to have any way to track you."

"Good Lord." *Was he serious? He looked like it.* She slowly closed her laptop. "So, when are we going someplace where I can send a few messages?"

"We're leaving on a commercial flight at noon today."

Feeling better, she set aside her laptop. "Right. Thank heavens for that."

"Maybe," he said cautiously. "You might not like what happens after that. We'll see how it goes."

She frowned at him. But he gave a small motion of his head, and she took that to mean, *Don't ask.* She groaned and said, "Whatever. How long until we leave?"

"We're not leaving for another hour," he said, "so, once you have more coffee, then we'll pack up and leave."

She nodded and pointed to her laptop. "Okay if I browse the internet?"

He nodded.

And she buried herself into catching up on the world news. But inside she couldn't help but wonder what was going on that Lennox wouldn't share with her yet. Still she was smart enough not to say anything.

LENNOX WAS GLAD that Helena had followed his cue and hadn't pushed for answers. He had a lot of discussions about flights going on right now. They needed to do a couple transfers to get back stateside. And that was a bit of an issue as well. The initial flights were booked and would take them to Holland. Lennox just wasn't sure where they were going from there. The next hour went very quickly.

Soon they had everybody packed up in a vehicle and heading to the airport. He already had extra alerts out. As they pulled into the airport, his phone buzzed. He took a look. And then swore and hit Dial. When Keane answered, Lennox said, "What the hell does that mean?"

"We've got two more boarding the same plane," he said, "both confirmed to have been part of that kidnapping scenario."

"Confirmed how?" Lennox asked, his temper thinning.

"Interpol had these two listed as known associates of the guy Carolina confirmed with the scars. We picked up their trail on a satellite. They've booked the same flight."

"Which means, we're not going on that flight."

"Exactly. That's changed. Now I need you to get out of the way and to keep out of sight."

"Are we still leaving from this airport?"

"Not anymore. Get back in the vehicle and follow the directions on the GPS." And he hung up.

Lennox took a look at the GPS, then turned to face the group. "Everyone, get back in the vehicle," and his tone brooked no resistance.

John immediately stepped back inside and said, "Why? I want to catch my flight!"

"We can't take the risk," Lennox snapped. "Our plan had been compromised."

"*Your* plan has been compromised?" Sasha said with a sneer. "What do I care? We don't have to go anywhere with you." She grabbed up her bag and marched toward the airport. John quickly followed her.

Lennox called out to them, "Two of the men who were part of your kidnapping have booked flights on the same flight as you will be on."

John frowned, looked at him, and asked, "So?"

"I highly suggest you don't share an airplane ride with them," Lennox said.

John shook his head as he followed Sasha. "You know what? We've been carted and packed and stuffed into various places for the last couple of days," he said, "and we just want to go home." As he held the entrance door open for Sasha, she waved at them with a big smile and cried out, "Good luck with whatever games you're playing." And they turned and both walked inside.

Carolina stepped up beside Lennox. "I guess we can't stop them, can we?"

He swore softly and steadily under his breath, barely even realizing what he was doing. "No, probably not," he said. "The trouble is, they're just two more pawns to be put into use. If somebody grabs them and tries to use them as hostages, what would you want me to do?"

"Well ..." And then she stopped. "I would still try to do

everything to keep them alive," she said slowly. "But what are we supposed to do if they don't want to listen, much less to cooperate? Believe me. Sharing that cage with them was no fun, what with all the complaining, whining, blaming."

"Exactly. It also means that, if Sasha and John are taken, we can't allow them to be used against us."

"Right. … Of course. … So, do *we* have another way to get back home again?" Helena asked, as she stared back at the airport, where the two were already walking toward the security checkpoint.

"We weren't expecting a change of plans right now."

"Yes, you were," she said. "You were at least expecting the possibility of it."

"Yes," he admitted. "Because nothing is set until it's actually done."

"Of course," Helena said.

"So, now what?" Carolina asked.

"Get back in the vehicle," he said. "We'll go to a different airport."

Without a word, the two women hopped back in.

With Helena's furtive glance at the airport and then at Gavin, he shrugged.

"We can't force them," he said, "and they might be just fine."

"And if they aren't?" Helena asked, looking back yet one more time.

Gavin's face turned grim. "And, if they aren't," he said, "it's not something we can do anything about now. This is not your fault. We've given them the best advice we could. It's ultimately their decision. They don't want to listen. It's pretty shitty, but it's also a lot easier on us if we're only looking after the two of you. And you both listen to us."

"I know that too, in theory," Lennox said, "but we had room for all six of us in our new plans."

"They don't seem to think that our plans matter," Gavin said calmly, "so we do what we have to do. Now let's go, before we don't make our own flights."

With a nod and an angry look at the airport, Lennox hopped in, and they drove off.

CHAPTER 10

"WHAT KIND OF plans do we have?" Helena asked.

"It'll be a bit of a hopscotch trip," he said, "but, once we realized that the kidnappers' associates had booked seats on the same flight, we knew we had to get you a long way away."

"I don't have a problem with that," she said, "but where are we flying to?"

"To England before we jump the pond," he said. "We were supposed to fly to Amsterdam first, but now we're flying to England, and then we'll see how we're getting across the ocean."

"Hopefully by plane," she said. "That's the fastest."

"It is," he said, "but it's not always the safest." And then, at that, he sat back and went quiet.

But she saw him always working on his phone, probably setting up the rest of their arrangements. She looked over at Carolina, one eyebrow up.

Carolina shrugged. "Trust in him. He's kept us safe so far."

And that was the part that bothered her. Why the hell had the other two not listened? It's not that she really expected the kidnappers to do anything, once they realized John and Sasha had split from Lennox. So there was a good chance that John and Sasha would both be fine, now that they weren't physically with Lennox, who was the kidnapper's ultimate target. But why would you take that chance alone, unarmed, and unskilled to handle those people? Helena shook her head.

Still, before long, they pulled up into a smaller airport and hopped into a private plane. She smiled as she saw it. "Now this is nice."

"It is," Lennox said. "We'll have to stop for refueling, and we'll probably do that in France."

"We could take another flight from France back the US," she said.

"Maybe. Let's keep to the schedule and see." He quickly loaded their duffel bags.

They boarded the flight and took off almost immediately. One good thing about private airplanes, like this one, was how much more comfortable boarding the planes were—simple, nothing involved. The conversation on the flight was pretty light as everybody avoided the topic of John and Sasha. And even of where they were going, although Gavin did ask Carolina what her future plans were, now that she had been kidnapped. Like, if she was leaving the doctor's program or if she would continue to work with the Red Cross.

"I'm not sure," Carolina said. "I was contemplating doing more traveling, but now I'm not certain I want to." She slid a glance at Gavin, and he nodded. "Particularly with Lennox's issue right now."

Gavin looked at Helena. "What about you?"

"I was looking at making a change too," Helena said quietly. "Carolina and I weren't traveling while we were married. And then, after our divorces, we both resumed traveling around the world again, more to escape than to start again. Now I'm almost ready to put down some roots."

"We've already talked about it a couple times," Carolina said, nodding at Helena. "It's just a matter of where and what's next for us."

"But the whole world is ahead of us," Helena said, comfortably rolling her head back, her eyelids heavy. "And I think I'm about ready to nod off and have a little bit of a nap. How long till we land?" Helena let her eyes close.

"We're not too far away from Paris now," Lennox said. "It won't be a long stop there either."

"Okay," she said. She looked at Carolina and asked, "Did you recognize any of the men that he showed you?"

"Yes," she said; then she frowned. "Did you hear us last night?"

Helena shrugged. "A little bit. Something about a bunch of faces."

"I could identify one kidnapper. The main guy in charge. With all the scars."

Helena looked at Lennox. "Did you know him?"

"No," he said, his tone terse.

Helena studied his face as he worked on a laptop. "You hadn't seen him *ever?*"

He lifted his gaze from the laptop, studied her for a long moment, then shook his head. "Not that I remember, no. And we're trained to remember faces, even when disguised. Even faces that have undergone cosmetic surgery. Because some things can't be changed."

"Like what?" Helena asked, intrigued.

"The distance between the eyes for one thing."

"Okay. … So why the hell would he be after …"

"I'm trying to figure that out," he said. "I'm backtracking his history to see where we might have met—or at least had crossed paths."

"Or," Carolina said brightly, "what if somebody else used your name?"

Instantly silence settled in the plane. "What do you mean?" Gavin asked.

Helena got it though. "What if," she said to Lennox, "somebody hated you. And then did something terrible and let everybody believe that he was you."

"Well, that would be a shitty thing to do," Gavin said.

"But we already know that this whole deal is a really shitty deal," Carolina said.

"Does somebody hate your guts enough to do something like this?" Helena asked. "This is pretty nasty to consider. But also, if you wanted to get somebody who you hated in big trouble, this was not a bad way to do it."

"I don't know," Lennox said, confusion in his gaze. "Let me think about it. You guys got off on a different angle, so leave me alone to find the connections."

Helena looked over at Carolina with a raised eyebrow.

Carolina shrugged and said, "Naptime." She stretched out in the airline seat and let her head drop against the window and closed her eyes.

"Not a bad idea," Helena said and curled up in the opposite seat, using her window as well as the sweater that she had brought with her, and fell asleep.

It wasn't very long before Lennox woke her up. She stared up at him in confusion, glanced around, and realized where she was again. "Are we here?"

"Yes," he said. "We're in Paris fueling up."

"Are we getting off?"

He shook his head. "No."

She glared at him. "Did you have a reason for waking

me then?"

He grinned. "Maybe to get up and walk around, shake your legs out a little bit."

"Or maybe just go back to sleep," she muttered and curled back up. She closed her eyes, and the next time she woke up, *again* she saw Lennox. She glared at him. "Seriously?"

His eyebrows shot up. "Now what?" he asked.

"Aren't we still in Paris?"

"No," he said, his smile kicking up the corners of his mouth. "We're in London now, not that it was much of an extra flight, but we needed the fuel."

"Fine," she replied, and then she realized what he said. "So we're here? Now we can go home? Can we get off?"

"We are getting off, but we're taking another flight across to the Maritimes."

"Why Canada?" she asked, running a finger through her hair.

"So we can connect to the coast."

She shrugged. "We can go the other way and go straight across to California."

"We could, but it'll take a long time."

"All of these hops are taking time." But she closed her mouth and just endured.

They did get off the plane and had about two hours before they hooked onto a commercial flight and ended up in Halifax, where they grabbed yet another flight that took them to Chicago. By the time they arrived in San Diego, she was tired, frustrated, and fed up. She looked at Carolina. "You know it would have been much nicer if we'd just gone to Munich."

She nodded. "It was supposed to be that way. This time

it'll be both of us at *your* apartment."

Helena shrugged listlessly. "It doesn't matter. We're here together now, I guess."

"Yeah, but I don't want to fly anymore for a while," Carolina groaned. "Oh, for a nice bed!"

"Well, we had one," she said. "Apparently staying in it wasn't to be."

They stood outside this final airport in the wee hours of the morning—something like two a.m. by the time they finally cleared customs, got their luggage, and everybody had gathered outside. She tried to shrug the cobwebs off her mind. And then realized Gavin was missing. She looked at Lennox. "Now what?"

"Well, it depends if you think it's safe enough to go to your apartment."

Her eyebrows shot up. "Why wouldn't it be?"

He shrugged. "Because it's still associated with you, and you're still associated with me."

"Well, how about your apartment?" she asked.

"That would be the worst place," he said.

Just then Gavin drove up. They all stared at the lime-green Jeep. "Hardly a very unassuming rental," Helena said, as she got in the back.

Gavin laughed. "This one is my own," he said. "I left it at the airport."

"That could have been a big bill," Lennox said, "depending how much longer we were detained overseas."

Gavin shrugged. "It's a huge boon having wheels available," he said. "You do what you have to do at the time." Gavin pulled away from the side strip and headed back onto the main freeway to leave the airport and to get out of the traffic. Even though it was the wee hours of the morning, still plenty of vehicles moved about.

"Where are we going?" Helena asked him.

"To a safe house," Gavin said.

"So not my place?"

Gavin shook his head. "No, we figured it was better to avoid all known places."

"And for how long?" she asked.

Lennox answered, "Until I can find out what's going on."

And she sat back and shared a hard look with Carolina. "That doesn't sound very promising."

"Do you want to live to see tomorrow?" Lennox turned around in the front seat to level a heavy stare at her.

She didn't have to answer that because, of course, she wanted to. But she didn't want to be in a cage either. She didn't know exactly what was going on, but, for the first time, she realized how John and Sasha felt. This was *his* problem, not their problem. She wouldn't throw him to the wolves, but, at the same time, this felt like something he needed to handle and fast. "Okay," she said, "you have three days."

At that, Gavin snorted, raised his gaze to the rearview mirror, and Lennox spun around again and glared at her. "What?"

"You've got three days," she announced, staring at him. "Three days to get this over with."

"Or then what?"

"Then I'm going back to my apartment," she said. "We're okay to hang out because we need a couple days just to chill anyway," she said. "But we have to move on. We can't just sit here and be sitting ducks."

"And how do you figure, by going back to your place,

that you *aren't* a sitting duck?"

"I don't know," she said, "but that's the time limit."

He shook his head and said, "It'll take as long as it takes." Lennox checked his phone and told Gavin, "Take the next left."

Gavin nodded and promptly pulled into the lane farthest away from any exit.

"And that will be *three days*," she said, her tone inflexible. Of course she couldn't force something like that to happen, but, if he didn't think there would be real consequences, then Lennox wouldn't move heaven and earth to fix this. And then she thought about that and shrugged. It was Lennox, of course, so he would move heaven and earth to fix it regardless. "And, if you need us, you have to speak up."

"And I would need you *why?*"

"Well, to start with," she said, "I'd like to see the face of this person who hates you so much. Because maybe, if we know him—or at least know what he looks like—that might let us tell you if we see him involved from here on out."

Lennox looked at her, startled for a moment, then brought up his phone and flicked through the recent images. And then he held up his phone, reached over the front seat to give it to her. "This is the guy I had problems with."

She looked at the man's image with one eyebrow shot up. She held it for Carolina to see it too, and they exchanged glances. Helena said, "Definitely not the kidnapper, but… well, we do know him. Can't say we like him either."

He looked at her in shock. "What do you mean, *you know him?*"

"He tried to date both of us," Helena said. "It was about two years ago maybe." She frowned, looking over at Carolina for confirmation, who just shrugged. Helena continued, "It was after we were both separated, but before we headed off, traveling with the Red Cross."

Gavin again changed lanes.

"Seriously?" Lennox glared at her. And then he spun to look at his sister.

She shrugged. "I didn't place him. I still don't remember him."

Lennox now faced Helena. "How often did you see him, and how pushy was he?" Lennox asked Helena.

"He was looking for information," Helena said, "but he seemed quite frustrated that we weren't cooperating."

"Interesting," Gavin said. "It's possible." He made the next left, as Lennox had instructed.

"It's bullshit is what it is!" Lennox said in disgust. "Just because he hates me doesn't mean that he would do something like this."

"No, but then, I hate to say it, why would he want to date me?" Carolina said. "Not that there's anything wrong with me, but I'm still your sister."

"But then maybe he didn't know that," Lennox said, grasping for straws.

"No," Helena said. "Rob knew because he's the one who said he was a friend of yours."

"Shit," Lennox said, looking out his passenger's side window. "The one thing he is *not* is a friend. And for him to have even said that is very suspicious right off the bat."

"Exactly," she said, "so I suggest that you check him out."

"What do you think I've been doing?" Lennox asked in exasperation.

"Aha," she said with a smile. "Like I said—*three days.*"

⚓

LENNOX WASN'T SURE how serious Helena was or whether she was just being snarky. He couldn't even imagine what he would have done if he'd found out Rob and Carolina—or Helena—were dating. He would have lost it big-time. "You've met him before," he said to Carolina, his arm slung across the front seat of Gavin's Jeep as he spoke to his sister.

Carolina looked at him and shook her head. "No, I haven't."

"You have," he said. "When I was on leave one day. Remember the guy who came to my door when you were over for dinner? And he tried to force his way in, and we had this big argument?"

She froze, looked at him, and said, "Yes, I do remember that. Not a lot. I didn't get a good look at him though."

"Well, that was him," he said shortly.

"Why does he hate you so much?"

"He raped a young girl over in Thailand, and I turned him in."

Silence.

"Okay then," Helena said softly. "Well, I guess he deserved that."

"If that's the case," Carolina said, "why the hell was he trying to date us a couple years ago?"

"He was drummed out of the military and jailed in Thailand," Lennox said. "I don't know what happened afterward. I lost track of him."

"That's all bullshit," Helena said. "Why the hell would he be allowed back on the streets?"

"He shouldn't be out of jail. Which is why I find it interesting that he tried to date both of you," he said, twisting to look at Helena. "Why would he try to date you too?"

She glared at him. "I don't know why."

Her tone was just caustic enough that he realized how his question came off. He rolled his eyes. "It's not like he would know there was anything between the two of us."

"Some people think there's more here than there is."

"Right," he said. He caught Gavin's questioning expression, and Lennox shrugged, shook his head. "No, we didn't have a thing. Just keep your eye on the road, please."

Carolina piped up. "They should have had a thing. It would have made them both easier to live with."

With that, Gavin started to chuckle. And then he laughed and laughed. "Okay," he said, "now I understand all the undercurrents."

"You do not," Helena muttered.

"No," Lennox said, under his breath. "You don't."

"Maybe not," Gavin said, still chuckling, "but I can guess. You really should go to a hotel and take care of business."

"Is that what having sex is to you?" Helena asked in an outraged voice. "*Taking care of business?*"

"Well, if it'll stop all this crackling resentment around us, then, yes," Gavin said. "You guys should have had a thing five years ago, and maybe you, Helena, wouldn't have gotten married, and you, Lennox, wouldn't have been lost for all these five years."

"How lost was he?" Carolina asked with interest.

Lennox smacked Gavin on the shoulder. "I was not lost," he announced. "Gavin is just being an ass."

"If you say so," he said and started to whistle. Unfortunately it was the wedding march. When he caught Lennox's gaze, Gavin roared with laughter.

"Glad you're having fun," Lennox muttered.

"Best I've had yet." He quickly changed lanes, moving into another.

"Why all the sudden lane changes?" Helena asked suspiciously.

"I just want to make sure we're not being followed," he said. "And—before you ask—no, we're not."

"God, I just want this over with."

"And it will be," Lennox said, "soon."

"Three days," she said darkly. "*Three days* or else …"

CHAPTER 11

HELENA WOKE THE next morning and froze, not recognizing the room. Her heart pounded, slamming against her chest, until she heard voices outside and recognized Lennox's. She groaned and sagged into the mattress, remembering that they were in a safe house. It was a rancher with lots of small bedrooms. They each had a bedroom; they each had a bed. Everybody was safe, and they weren't all that far away from her own apartment. Maybe twenty minutes if she drove and maybe an hour if she walked.

She got up, slowly walked into the bathroom, yawning. She only had her clothes in her travel bag, so at least enough for a week's holiday. But this was a long way away from a holiday. She closed the bathroom door, hopped into the shower, and, when she felt more refreshed, she stepped out, dried off, and dressed. She pulled out her dirty clothes, wondering if a washing machine was here.

With all her clothes laid out on the bed, she looked at the dresser and decided that, since she was here for almost three days, she might as well unpack. With everything removed, her dirty laundry to the side, she put her empty carry-on bag into the closet and then walked into the kitchen. "I guess this layout makes sense if it's a safe house," she said, "but, if it were my place, I would want my bedroom twice as big."

"I think they took the bedrooms and cut them in half just for that reason, so they could pack in more people," Gavin said without looking up. He motioned at the coffeemaker and said, "That's the second pot. You may want to get a cup now."

"Wow," she said, "have you already drunk a whole pot yourself?"

"Nope," he said, "Lennox has been helping me."

"Is Carolina up?"

"Yep, you're the last one, sleepyhead."

She chuckled. "I finally slept though. I feel one hundred times better."

"Good," he said, "so you'll have some patience when Lennox doesn't finish this job in three days."

"Nope," she said, as she sat down and reached for a section of the newspaper. "He's got three days. Now he's got half a day less."

Gavin let out a bark of laughter. "Well, you're nothing if not a hard-ass."

"If you want to get shit done," she said, "you have to have deadlines and discipline, and you got to make your goals."

"And so is your goal his goal?"

She stopped, frowned at him. "What does that mean?"

Gavin shook his head. "You make your goals," he said, "but that doesn't mean they're Lennox's goals too."

"Maybe not," she said, "but obviously we've been on his enemy's target list for a while."

"And I wanted to ask you more details about that," Lennox said, as he walked in to join them.

Carolina walked in beside him, came over, and hugged Helena. "You look much better."

"What kind of details?" Helena asked.

Carolina pulled up a chair beside Helena, the two women close as always. They both looked at Lennox with quizzical glances.

"How did he find you?"

"I remember him now. We were at a coffee shop," Carolina said promptly. "He walked up, introduced himself as one of your friends, and said that he happened to be around and recognized me."

"And how did you know that he was telling the truth?"

"Because he knew something about your place," she said. "Mentioned that you guys had done a couple missions together and also mentioned a couple other friends that you have in common who I also knew."

"Right, so confidence-building, letting you know that he really does belong in my world. So why didn't you guys go out with him?"

"You mean, besides the fact that we were both not going out with men at all then?" Carolina asked.

Lennox nodded.

"I can answer that," Helena said. "I didn't like something about him. I don't want to say that I saw a 'violent edge' to him, but something was in his gaze. It was just wrong."

"*Wrong?*" Gavin said slowly, as he put down the newspaper and looked at her. "Wrong, how?"

"Cold. Dead. As if something was going on in there that was completely disconnected from the world around us."

"Interesting assessment," Lennox said. "Gavin, you know him too, don't you?"

"I do," Gavin said. "And she's right. There's a coldness in him."

"Then our instincts were a whole lot better that time," she added, with a knowing look at Carolina. "I haven't seen him since though."

"Is that the only time he approached you?"

"No, we saw him several times throughout that week," she said. She frowned and looked at Carolina. "I think it's because of him that we switched coffee shops, wasn't it?"

Carolina looked thoughtful, as if casting her mind back. "You know what? I think it was. We went there every morning at nine a.m. to catch up," she said slowly to the men. "We needed that. Even though we probably spoke for four hours every evening, it was that physical contact that we needed with each other to get through the day back then. But Rob was disturbing," she admitted.

"I think we went to a coffee shop around the corner and then saw him again, and so we stopped our coffee shop ritual. Instead we ended up picking up coffee somewhere else and walking down on the beach."

"Right," Carolina said. "The more we distanced from him, the angrier he seemed to be, which then made us distance even more."

"Exactly." Helena agreed with a solemn nod.

"Did he ever follow you home?" Lennox asked.

"How would we know?" Helena asked. "We left soon afterward with the Red Cross."

"So, if Rob had any plans," Carolina said, "we probably ruined them right away."

"And it might have taken time for him to figure out just where and what you two were up to."

"Exactly. But when scar-man found us, apparently Rob had found us in a big way," Helena said. "Do you think he would have done something to this guy using your name?"

"It's possible," Lennox said. "I can't tell you what other people have done. I can tell you that I don't know who this guy with the scar is. As far as I know, I've never met or done anything to him."

"And this guy—Rob, your friend or not—what was his real name?"

"Just call him Rob," he said. "I think his real name is Robert McMillan or something."

"And did you find very many places where you crossed paths with Rob?"

"None that matter," he said. "They were all before he was charged."

"What about this scarred guy?"

"No way to know. But he was, as far as I can tell, in Thailand for a long time. So our time there could have overlapped."

"Do you think he would know the girl who Rob raped?" Helena asked.

Both men looked at her with added respect.

She shrugged. "I'm just looking for a link. The other problem is, if Rob did this once, what are the chances he did it again?"

"So you think that, maybe instead of something this Rob guy did directly to the man with the scar, Rob might have done something to somebody close to the man with the scar?" Gavin asked Helena.

"I don't know," she said tiredly. "You're making my brain hurt."

"You're the med school student with the 99.9% ranking, which probably will never be usurped," Lennox said, scoffing. "Your brain only hurts when it doesn't have a million things to work on."

She shot him a look. "My brain always intimidated you," she announced. "That's probably why you didn't want to go out with me."

Silence fell at the table. And then once again, Gavin chuckled. "As I said," he said, "you two need to spend some time together."

"Nope," she said. "We already spent some time together."

"Didn't go so well, huh?" Gavin asked.

Lennox glared at her. "Go ahead. Why don't you just air all our dirty laundry?"

"I would, but there isn't any to air," she said blithely, as she waved a hand in his direction. "That's the problem with nonstarters."

He gave her a loud snort. "Nothing happened."

"Nope," she said, "one crazy-wild kiss, and both of us backed off, deciding that it wasn't what we wanted at the time."

"And all because of me too," Carolina said. "Right?" The two of them exchanged looks, looked at her, and Carolina nodded. "I knew that's what you were doing. I kept telling you both it was okay."

"But it's not okay," Helena said, "because I wasn't prepared to jeopardize our relationship."

Carolina grabbed her best friend's fingers and said, "Why would you think a relationship with my brother, even if you two broke up, would jeopardize us?"

"Because it happens," she said, "and you're too important to me."

"You were just scared," Carolina said. "Admit it. You were afraid that Lennox was too good to be true."

At that, Helena laughed. "Well, he isn't, so it all worked

out."

Just then, his phone rang. Lennox pulled it out, checked the number, and answered it. "Keane, what's up?"

She looked over at Gavin. "Who's Keane?"

"One of our team who runs the communication center."

"Cool," she said, studying Gavin's face. Then she looked over at Lennox and said, "Or not cool."

Gavin nodded. "It looks like *not cool* to me as well."

"HE ARRIVED IN the US? San Diego? Walked right through security?"

"Apparently," Keane said. "He wasn't supposed to be let in without questioning."

"He was involved in the kidnapping and a hostage scenario. How the hell was he allowed to enter the country?"

"We're still investigating all that," Keane said. "The whole point of this call is to tell you to watch your back." And he hung up.

"So our scarred man is Stefano Hartland, both on his birth certificate and on his current IDs," Lennox said to the three staring at him in shock. "And he arrived two hours ago in the US. He's already cleared customs, and they're just now getting around to telling us."

"Wow," Helena said. "I thought we were all on the same team."

"The teams are variable obviously," he said. He glared at his phone. "So I want to get into the security in your apartment building to see if he's figured out where you are, and then there's my sister." He looked at her. "You don't have a place here any longer, do you?"

She shook her head. "No, just the one in Munich."

"So, if you were to come here, where would you stay?"

"If not with you, with Helena of course," she said.

"So we're back to Helena." Lennox worked away on his laptop, checking for cameras and security systems. "You have a high-end security system at your place."

"Well, as good as I could get," she said. "It's a new apartment for me, after I divorced."

He looked up and realized why she'd have extra security on her place, and he approved. But he hated the reason behind it. "I'll need permission from you and the building's owner to get into the system."

"Or you don't get permission," she said. "You can get in there anyway."

He immediately opened the chat window and asked for access to the building's security feeds. It took at least three minutes, and then a link popped up.

"And I'm in," he said, with a note of satisfaction. He really loved this Mavericks system. He worked his way back to this morning's video, checking to make sure that nobody suspicious had come or gone. "Nobody's been there so far today."

"That you know of," Helena said. "What if your other idiot, Rob, set up something beforehand?"

Lennox sat back, looked at her, and asked, "What are you thinking?"

"I don't know," she said, staring at him, and he saw the fear lurking in the back of her eyes. "But just to think that this guy even knows where I live won't help me sleep at night."

"Which is why," he said, "we have to find him."

"I get that," she said, "but this isn't exactly helping

now."

"It is if we can figure out if he's found your place or not."

"Why don't you go back a couple days?" Carolina asked. "See if Rob showed up early."

"No reason for him to," Gavin said, shaking his head, "but this whole thing has been one messed-up illogical incident." He had his laptop out too. The two of them worked away, checking on the various camera feeds.

And then Lennox froze. He tapped Gavin and said, "See if you can get a better picture of this guy." And he gave him the time and date.

With the second laptop, Gavin opened up angles from the other cameras. "Well, look at that," he said. "Rob." And he pointed out the stranger with a baseball cap and sunglasses.

"And how do you know it's Rob?" Helena asked, hopping up and running around to see him. Carolina followed.

Lennox pointed to the scar and the slightly distorted tattoo on the back of his hand. "Rob was injured with several bullets and some shrapnel in one of the missions, and it buggered up that tattoo."

"So this was what? Four days ago?" Helena asked.

Lennox and Gavin both nodded.

"So why is he in my apartment building back then?" As they all watched the replay, Rob headed toward an apartment on the main floor and, with keys, let himself in. "That son of a bitch has an apartment in the same building?" she cried out in outrage.

"Appears to be true," Lennox said quietly. "So now the question is, *Why?*"

"Well, it's too much of a coincidence to think that he

didn't have a long-term plan for this," Gavin said. "So he's there because she's there."

"I don't understand why it's me though," Helena stated, staring from Lennox to Gavin and back.

"Because, like I said, that's the only place I would go," Carolina said. "Although we *were* going to Munich."

"Except," Helena said, as she sat back down again, "we were originally going home to San Diego," she said, "and then we changed our plans."

"So who would know your original plans and then wouldn't have realized when you made a change of plans?" Lennox asked Helena and his sister.

"I don't know," Helena said, staring at him in shock. "We talked about it while we were at work all the time. Any number of people could have heard us."

"But who would care?" Lennox asked, pressing the women. "That's the real question."

Both women shrugged. "I have no idea," Helena stated.

"I wonder if he's still there," Gavin said thoughtfully. "Maybe he's living there."

Lennox shot him a hard look. "I suggest we go find out."

Immediately Helena jumped to her feet. "I want to go too."

"Well, that's not happening," Lennox said, with a glare in her direction.

She glared right back. "It's my apartment!"

"No," he said, "it's his apartment."

"So what does that mean though?" she asked. "Why would he be watching me?"

"To find me," Carolina said. "And, therefore, ultimately to find Lennox."

"So what about this other guy who landed at the airport?

Stefano?" Helena asked the guys.

"For all we know, he's part of whatever this angle Rob is working," Lennox said.

"Maybe they're working together on both ends. The kidnapping first and now Rob's part. Maybe Rob was lying to you," Gavin said to the women. "People lie all the time, particularly when it diverts attention away from them."

Lennox frowned. "Anything's possible." He hopped up and said, "Gavin, stay here with the women?"

"Absolutely. What about weapons?"

"Right, we had to leave the others behind." He stopped and looked around.

"Exactly, so now we're stuck."

"Or not," Lennox said, his mind buzzing. He sent a message to Keane, almost laughing when he got an immediate response to check out the back of the master closet. He loved this team.

Before Lennox took off, Helena stopped him with a look. "Wait. Talk to me."

Lennox sat down, knowing he had an arsenal at his disposal just feet away from him, so he had some time to spare.

"What does any of that have to do with my apartment?"

"Maybe nothing," Lennox said. He looked at Gavin, his fingers spinning his pen back and forth, back and forth again. "We need to pull in some information on what Rob has been doing since his incarceration, how he got out so fast. And see if this other guy with the scars has any connection with Coronado."

"Different country," Gavin said. "Digging won't be easy."

"I know," Lennox said. "But something else is going on here, unless it's just as simple as grabbing Carolina again—or maybe both of them—because where else would my sister and Helena go at this point?"

"*Anything* is possible at this point," Gavin said with a sigh. "We know more but not near enough. Yet."

"I know," Lennox said. Frowning, he looked at the women and said, "I need you guys to disappear."

"We're in a safe house already. They should be fine," Gavin noted.

Lennox looked at Gavin, shaking his head, and said, "This Stefano guy got into the States easily enough. Not one border crossing question made. He bypassed US Navy orders. What do you think the chances are that Stefano knows about this safe house?"

"If he has access to satellite, like we do, Stefano—or Rob—could have tracked my vehicle," Gavin admitted. "It's in the garage right now, but that doesn't mean they didn't see it earlier."

"Exactly." And Lennox's instincts rode him hard. "I don't like it," Lennox said. "Pack up and be ready to leave in fifteen."

He bolted to his feet and raced to the bedroom.

CHAPTER 12

HELENA LOOKED AT Gavin. "Is he serious?"

But he was already nodding. "Move," he said, "now." There was a definite bite to his tone. The two women got up, and Helena muttered as she headed to her bedroom, "I just unpacked."

"Well, something set both of them off, but I don't know what," Carolina said.

"At this point, probably just gut instincts," Helena said, as she grabbed all her clothing from the dresser and picked up her dirty laundry. "I was going to ask if they had washing machines here so I could do a little laundry."

"Me too," Carolina said.

Quickly both women had everything packed up. Helena used the washroom for good measure and then stepped out into the kitchen with her carry-on bag and asked, "Where are we going?"

The look she got from Gavin was *Keep an open mind.*

"If you say so," she said. And the two of them headed out to the Jeep in the garage.

Very quickly they were back on the road—Lennox looking behind them often, while Gavin changed lanes more times than needed—but they headed into the Coronado base.

She frowned. "You think we'll be safer on the base? This

Stefano guy just waltzed into our country."

But, instead of stopping there, they moved to the pier and out to a wharf. At the end was a small boat where they were putting in their bags.

"Isn't this taking things a little far?" Helena whispered to Carolina, as they all headed out to a naval ship. Not a big one but a small one. "What is this?"

"A safe place for you to stay while we go to town on these two guys," Lennox said, and, sure enough, the women were lifted to the bottom rung, handed up, and, once on top of the deck, were moved off to an officer. He saluted to both Gavin and Lennox, still in the transport boat, before the women were escorted inside.

Lennox and Gavin took the skiff right back to shore.

Once inside, Helena looked around and said, "I'm sorry to be such a bother."

The officer smiled at her. "And I'm quite happy to have the company. Most of the men are on shore leave," he said, "so we have a skeleton crew. But you're more than welcome to stay." He led them to a small room with a top and bottom bunk and said, "This is yours, for the moment."

"I don't suppose the guys gave you any idea how long we would be here, did they?"

"For the day, possibly overnight," he said, "so make yourself at home."

Helena nodded and said, "And I hate to be a pain, but we didn't get a chance to eat. Is there a possibility of a coffee at least?"

His face broke into a big smile. "And that will make the cooks happy," he said. "So, if you're ready to drop your bags, we'll take you down and get you some breakfast."

And that's what they did. The whole time she looked

around with interest. She didn't imagine too many civilians were treated to a first-hand look at the inside of one of these cruisers. She kept peppering the officer with questions about how many men it took to run the ship and how far they could go on the fuel tanks, all kinds of stuff, because her mind just wouldn't let up on it.

Finally he stopped, looked at her, and asked, "Are you writing a book or something?"

Carolina laughed and said, "You have to understand that my friend's mind doesn't stop. She's constantly barraging all of us for more information. She reads tour books and encyclopedias."

The officer looked at her in surprise.

Helena shrugged. "I have an unending thirst for knowledge, particularly all sorts of minutia," she said with a grin.

He led them into a large open room and up to a large counter. He called out and said, "We have two special visitors for the next twenty-four hours, and they're hungry."

A massive guy on the backside with an apron wrapped around his waist gave the women a meaty grin and said, "Perfect! I hope you guys can eat."

"I can eat," Helena said. "Hard to get full actually."

"Watch what you say," the officer said. "Fill them up, Miko."

And they were led to a large selection of food, where they got to order exactly what they wanted. With trays laden down, everything from sausages and eggs and hash browns to fried tomatoes and half of a muffin filled with cheese on the side, topped off with a full cup of fresh coffee. The officer led them to a lovely table by the window and said, "Here's a seaside view for you."

As she sat down, Helena exclaimed over the view. "Oh, wow," she said, "this is beautiful."

He asked, "Do you mind if I join you?"

They looked at him in surprise, and both said, "No, of course not. Please do."

When he returned with his coffee, then Helena remembered her manners. "I'm sorry," she said. "I didn't introduce myself. I'm Helena."

"And I'm Carolina, Lennox's sister," Carolina piped up.

He smiled, shook both their hands, and said, "And I'm Ben," he said. "It's nice to have you two aboard. It can get annoyingly boring here at times."

"I imagine it can when you're just sitting around, filling the time," she said with a smile. "But I'm also sure there's never enough downtime so it's a welcome relief."

"Absolutely," he said.

The next hour passed in the beautiful daze of socializing and visiting as Helena plowed through a ton of food. Carolina's plate was half the size. But then Carolina was much smaller. Helena looked at her friend and said, "We ended up in sunshine and roses after all."

"We deserve it," Carolina said complacently.

Ben asked, "What do you two do?"

Helena looked at him and smiled and said, "We're doctors," she said. "We've just come back from a Red Cross trip." When she glanced at Carolina, silently asking for permission, Helena shrugged and added, "We were kidnapped. We just landed in San Diego, and our friends were looking for a safe place to stash us as they hunt down the kidnappers."

At that, the officer said, "I didn't get any intel on why," he said, "but that makes perfect sense. Are both of you doctors?"

Carolina launched into a tale about how they've been best friends since grade school and how they'd made a pact to become doctors and to help the world.

"Wow," he said. By then a couple other officers joined them. Everybody sat at the table, enjoying the discussion about how Carolina's and Helena's lives had gone from grade school to med school to being kidnapped. Helena smiled. "I don't even know that we're supposed to talk about it, but Lennox didn't tell me not to. Although he doesn't say very much."

"Lennox is like that," another man said as he approached the table.

She looked up, realized it was the captain. And she stood and shook his hand. "Thank you very much for keeping us for the day," she said in a formal note.

He smiled and said, "It's nice to have some fresh faces aboard."

And that set the tone for the rest of the day. They got a full tour of the cruiser, and later they ended up back at their room, with access to their laptops and internet. It was a lovely day. When Helena's phone rang, she looked down and didn't recognize the number. "Hello?"

"It's me," Lennox said.

"Did you catch him?" Helena asked instantly, putting the laptop off to the side of her bunk. Carolina immediately joined her, and Helena put her phone on Speaker. "Carolina is here with me too."

"Your kidnapper, Stefano, was seen at your apartment," he said. "We just missed him." His voice was frustrated and angry.

"And Rob?"

"His apartment is empty and had been cleaned out."

"Go check mine," she said.

"Are you okay with that?" he asked. "I need to take a look to see if he's been in your place at all."

"Do it," she said. "I didn't give you the key though."

"Don't worry about that," he said quickly. "I can get in without it."

"Fine," she said, "but then you'll get back to me and let me know what you find."

"Will do," he said, and he hung up.

She looked at Carolina. "Maybe this is progress."

LENNOX GLARED AT Gavin. "How could we have missed him?"

"I'm not even sure we did," Gavin said, studying the outside of the apartment building. "Do we know for sure he traveled alone?"

"No, not necessarily. We have a lot of videos still to go through. The Mavericks in command central are working on it now."

"You think Stefano's visit was a decoy of some kind? So we're watching him when Rob is up to something?"

Lennox nodded, his mouth a grimace. "We never see Stefano and Rob together on the tapes."

"Not so far," Gavin agreed.

"I think the bottom line is, we need to get into her apartment."

"Do you really think Stefano or Rob have gone in there?"

"Why wouldn't they have?" Lennox said.

"Aren't they looking for you? And, if we go in there, we're playing into their hands."

"Right," he said, "that's possible."

"I know," Gavin said, "and yet I guess this is our best chance to find either of them."

They made their way inside up to the second floor, where Helena's apartment was. They walked down the hallway to see eight doors on each side. It wasn't a big building, relatively small for the area, and security was pretty high-end. Once you got inside, cameras were on both ends of both floors. It didn't mean a whole lot though.

Lennox walked up to Helena's apartment, took out his pick, and quickly unlocked the door. They stepped inside, and immediately Lennox held up a finger. Gavin nodded. Lennox slipped out of his shoes, closed the door quietly, and stepped through to the living room.

Instantly he was faced with her kidnapper; anger surged through him. He glared at the intruder. "What are you doing here?"

With a handgun in one hand and what looked like a set of handcuffs in the other, the kidnapper's intention was pretty obvious. Stefano just grinned at Lennox and said, "I'm looking for someone. But you're not that someone."

"How do you know I'm not?" Lennox challenged.

"I'm looking for Lennox," Stefano said. "You're not him."

And that's when Lennox realized this *was* a case of mistaken identity. "Actually I *am* Lennox," he said slowly, "but I suspect the person you are looking for is Rob."

The man's face twisted with rage. "You can't tell me what I know and what I don't know!" he said. "Where are the women?"

"What women?"

The kidnapper made a broader arm sweep. "The one who lives here."

"Ah, Helena?" At the man's nod, Lennox said, "She is safe. Along with Carolina."

Stefano frowned. "Yes, his sister."

"Yes," Lennox said. "*My* sister."

"You are not him," Stefano said, his voice harsh, his fist tightening on the handgun.

"Well, how did you know that she was my sister?"

"I have informants," he said.

"You didn't confirm it yourself?"

The man slowly shook his head. "No," he said, "my information has always been excellent."

"Well, I'm Lennox," he said, "but I don't know you at all."

The man's gaze narrowed at him.

"I'm going to take my phone out of my pocket," Lennox said. "Okay?"

With the handgun still pointed in his direction, Stefano nodded.

Lennox pulled out his phone quickly, pulled up a picture of Rob, and said, "I presume you know what the guy you're looking for looks like?"

Again the intruder nodded.

"Is this him? I call him Rob." And he held up Rob's photo.

The man glared at it and said, "Yes, but that's not Rob. That's Lennox."

"No, it is not," he said again. "I'm Lennox, and this is Rob."

Stefano shook his head.

Just then Gavin stepped around the side of Lennox, and Stefano turned his gun on him too. But Gavin stood close and said, "You're wrong. This is Lennox. And I can prove it."

Stefano glared at him. "How will you prove it?"

Gavin pulled out his phone and said, "Take a look at this picture." It was a photo of Lennox, still in his Navy SEAL uniform, being handed an award.

Stefano looked at Lennox and frowned. "This can't be Lennox." But his voice was confused, his face twisted with fury, as if fearing a trick. But, instead of accepting it, he looked angrier. "This is not true!" he said. "I was told it was you."

"*Told?*" Lennox pounced. "Told what? By whom?"

But Stefano reached up and once again touched the burn mark on his neck, the same tell as Helena had described.

Lennox held his hands out. "I get that you've got something against someone," he said, "but I think you have it against the wrong person."

Instead of listening to Lennox, the intruder shook his head, waving the gun around. "That can't be true!"

"Why not?"

"Because the one is a friend," he said. "And you are not him."

"I don't understand," Lennox said.

"I got the information from a friend," he reiterated. And then he took several steps back, heading toward the patio.

"Look. My sister is Carolina," Lennox said. "I don't have a birth certificate here with me, but I have a family tree. I have all kinds of proof that I am Lennox," he said. "So, if it's me you're looking for, then tell me what your beef is?" he asked. "Otherwise, somebody is using my name and blaming me for something I didn't do."

The guy gave him a haunted look and was suddenly gone through the double patio doors.

Lennox raced after Stefano to find the guy already gone. Lennox stood here, studying the layout, and looked back at Gavin, but he had gone out the front door.

It made no sense. Well, it was starting to make some sense. Somebody—Rob—had chosen to blame Lennox and had given this Stefano guy a target for whatever rage and revenge fantasy he had in his mind.

But they needed Stefano to understand it wasn't Lennox who was to blame. As he turned to walk back inside, he came face-to-face with Rob.

He leaned against the open front door, one foot in Helena's apartment, the other in the hallway, and said, "Wow, you're still alive. I'm surprised."

"No thanks to you," Lennox snapped. "Are you the one behind all this madness?"

"Behind all what?" he asked innocently, yet sported a big grin on his face. "What are you doing here with her?"

"Who is *her*?" Lennox asked.

"Helena, of course. I moved close so I could get to know her. I can't say I'm too thrilled if you are hanging around, hooking up with her."

Lennox stared at him in shock and confusion. "What the hell are you talking about?"

But Rob appeared to be stuck in his fantasy world. "Helena asked me to move closer," he said, "so that we could spend more time together."

"What?"

"Or is she stringing both of us along?" Rob said. "Ask her."

"You ask her," Lennox said, frowning at Rob. He didn't know what the hell was going on, but Stefano and now Rob were not acting normal or sanely.

"She is going out with me," Rob said slowly. "So I'm assuming you're here on a visit because of her best friend, Carolina, your sister. How is that going? I just want to make sure that it's platonic because I won't take kindly to her having an affair with you."

"She's not having an affair with you," Lennox said, feeling something twist inside him. What was going on? "She can't stand the sight of you." And he shouldn't have said that because rage lit up Rob's eyes. "What is this all really about? And what did you have to do with that guy who just was in here?"

"I don't know what you're talking about," Rob said, and he turned to shut the door and walked away. Immediately Lennox stepped out in the hallway to see Rob disappearing down the stairs to his floor. Lennox followed him. "Rob, what's going on?"

"Nothing," he said, "except that you need to be out of the picture, and I plan on moving into Helena's place."

"Why would you be moving into Helena's place?"

Rob turned to look at him and said, "Because we're meant to be together."

"When did you see her last?" Lennox asked curiously, trying to understand what was going on in Rob's psyche.

"Well, I stop in whenever I can," he said, "but it hasn't been enough. It's been years since we've spent much time together," he said. "But she's left the Red Cross, so we can spend a lot more time together."

Wow. He thinks she would leave the Red Cross because of the kidnapping? Or was this just his mind stuck in a fantasy world? "But you had to get rid of me first, is that it?" Lennox asked cautiously.

"Well, I was planning on getting rid of you anyway," he said, "but this is a good way to do it."

"If we were talking about Carolina, then that would make sense. But why Helena?"

"What do you mean, *why Helena?*" Rob asked. "She's my girlfriend."

"Since when?" Lennox asked, quietly feeling as if his whole world had dropped out of focus. He didn't understand what the hell was going on, but too many different stories overlapped and yet conflicted, and nothing about this was normal. Rob was calm, acting natural, but the words coming out of his mouth were anything but.

"Since you walked away and didn't want her," Rob said. "Thank you for that."

He stared and frowned at Rob. "When did you last see her and me together?"

"Must have been about five years by now," Rob said. "You know we were pretty good friends, and I was pretty sure that I could show her the light, but then you turned out to be an asshole and got me into all kinds of trouble."

"You raped a young girl," Lennox said, his fists clenched as he remembered that nightmare time. "Did you actually see Helena and me together?"

"Sure," he said. "That was one hell of a kiss, dude."

He realized that kiss had been somewhat public. It's one of the reasons why they had distanced themselves afterward because that had been just too hot, too fiery, and had also gotten out of control too fast. "So you were at that party?"

"Of course. We went everywhere together back then, until you turned around and betrayed me." Rob gave a harsh laugh. "You got amnesia? Sounds like you don't remember anything. Too bad your memory wasn't as shitty back then. I'd have been fine."

"So you were behind the kidnapping?"

"More or less," he said, "but I didn't want the women hurt. I'd never do anything to hurt Helena."

"But somebody must be feeding you information."

"Sure," he said, "and, if you haven't figured that out yet, that's pretty damn sad too. You used to be smarter."

"I haven't figured anything out," Lennox said quietly, as he studied the obviously unbalanced man in front of him. "What happened to you?"

"Well, I was in jail in Thailand," he said. "After the military court-martialed me, they turned me over to the Thai police, as they considered it their crime, and I was there until I bought my way out."

"How the hell did you buy your way out?" Lennox stared at him in disbelief. That's not what he'd hoped to hear.

"We can buy anything over there. The guy who's after you is the one who paid for my release."

"What the hell?" Lennox said in shock. "Why would he do that?"

Rob shot him a cocky grin and said, "Jesus, you're even stupider than I thought," he said. "You're just not getting it." Then he laughed and said, "Don't worry about it."

Just then a crowd of people moved into the apartments. And Rob took that opportunity to duck into his apartment.

The crowd quickly swept past Lennox when he tried to get through them to get into Rob's place. When he finally turned the knob, the door was locked. He pulled his pick out and entered as soon as he could and ran inside, but he found no sign of Rob.

The glass doors to the ground floor patio were open, and he was gone.

CHAPTER 13

THE WOMEN WERE back in their bunks, alone in their assigned room, when a hard knock came at the door.

"Hello?" Helena asked, as she hopped from the bottom bunk.

"It's me," Lennox said.

She opened the door in surprise, and he looked to see his sister sound asleep. "I've got a room across the hall here. Come over and let's talk, so we don't wake her."

Helena shrugged and said, "Fine." Dressed in a camisole and shorts, still she was decently covered, only it felt more intimate than it should. As she headed to his room, she realized he had a place all to himself. "This is dangerous," she murmured, closing the door behind her.

"No," he said, "not really." Lennox sagged on the floor and said, "A lot of really crazy shit is going on."

She wrapped up in the blanket on top of his bunk and said, "Tell me."

"I've already shared it with Gavin, and he's gone to rest. To let his brain shut down," he said, "because we can't figure out what's going on."

"Well, talk to me as well," she said, "although it might be better if Carolina was here too."

"Well, it seems like this wasn't about Carolina as much as it was about you."

Her jaw dropped. "Who the hell cares about me?"

"Rob," Lennox said quietly. And he slowly explained what had gone down at her apartment.

She shook her head. "So not only my kidnapper was there but Rob is still living in the same building? And he came up while you were there?"

"Yes," he said.

"But I thought his apartment was empty. … You know that makes no sense, right?"

"I hear you," he said, "but honestly, at this point, nothing makes sense." He continued with the rest of the story.

"What are you talking about, that I have a relationship with him? And was he there at the party? Back then?"

"Apparently," he said. "Although I don't remember too much about the circumstances."

"Well, a lot of military personnel and doctors were there," she said. "You brought the military, and I brought a lot of the medical staff."

"I remember that much," he said. "I guess it's possible Rob was there and that Rob did see the kiss."

"So he arranges to get you out of my life so he can have me?" She shook her head. "That doesn't compute. I get a vote as to whether I date someone or not. What does this asshole have to do with the kidnapping?"

"The kidnapping was to get me out of your life, courtesy of Stefano, so Rob could have you, as well as payback for Rob being court-martialed and then in jail."

"But Rob's the one who raped that girl."

"He says it was consensual. But, yes, she was younger, and she was beaten up pretty bad."

"And he says that you're to blame?"

"Well, if I had turned a blind eye to it," he said, "Rob

would still have his military career."

"Instead he was court-martialed and turned over to the Thai police to stand trial, is that correct?"

"According to what he said, yes, and there he somehow managed to get a connection to the kidnapper, who bought his release."

"Well, for whatever reason, the kidnapper needed a target, and Rob gave it to him."

"That's what I'm thinking, but, whether they were in jail together or whether somebody who knew Stefano was in jail with Rob, I don't know."

And, indeed, Lennox looked completely pissed and angry.

"The minute you suggested that somebody else was putting me forth as the bad guy, Rob is the one who came up in my mind."

"That guy is just an asshole and crazy to boot," she said. "He'd be a natural suspect for anybody's enemy."

Lennox laughed. "He was back then, and he still is."

"So I guess we're staying here then," she said, looking around the ship.

"Unless you don't want to. I can't force you to stay here. Plus the longest we can hide you here is another day and a half before the ship leaves the port."

"I can't even believe that Rob's saying all this. What a liar." That Rob would make up such lies, especially to Lennox, irritated her. Thankfully she and Carolina had already explained their feelings about Rob to Lennox. "You didn't believe him, did you?"

"No, of course not, but he did look …" Lennox hesitated.

"What?"

"He did look unsettled, as in potentially not quite all there right now. I don't know what to say. He didn't look like I expected him to look."

"You were friends for a long time, correct?"

"Not good friends but friends, yes. After all, we were both in the navy," Lennox said. "He seems to think we hung out all the time together." Lennox shook his head. "It's unfortunate to see what's happening to him right now."

"I think it comes back to the simplest of things," she said. "Whether it involves me or not, he's all about getting back at you. If he takes you out, then he thinks that'll leave me free and clear, and, if I matter to you, having me to himself makes him that much happier too."

"I don't understand that," he said, "because it was just a kiss."

"For you and me it was just a kiss. We allowed ourselves to block it out and to believe it was just a kiss. But apparently, to everybody else around us, it wasn't just a kiss."

"Right," he said. He stopped, looked at her quietly. "And so, for you, was it just a kiss?"

She laughed. "That's what we agreed it would be."

"And I think we also discussed the fact that neither of us was necessarily prepared to leave that decision in the past where it belongs."

"No," she said, "but this is hardly the time to reopen that discussion."

"Well, I've got an idea," he said suddenly, as he stood up.

"Oh?" she said, looking up at him from the bunk. "What's that?"

"Why don't we try it again?"

"No," she said, "that's not cool."

"Afraid?"

"Of course I'm afraid," she said. "You know what I've been through these last few days. Hell, these last few years."

He stopped, appeared to think about it, then nodded. "So maybe a kiss for comfort?"

"Hell, no," she said, but she could feel the fear inside her. Not of him but of what could happen if they came together again.

"Would it be that bad?"

"This is ridiculous," she groaned, blowing the hair back out of her face, trying to keep him on track. "So Rob what? He sees our kiss and thinks that maybe it would be like that with him and me?"

"Maybe," he said. "Unfortunately it was right before he raped that girl. It might have pushed him into that direction."

"When you were in Thailand? It was then?" She didn't understand the undercurrents.

Lennox nodded. "Maybe you don't remember the exact timing of the party," he said, "but I was leaving the next day."

"Oh, shit!" she said. "Now I do remember." She thought about it and remembered how desperately she'd wanted him. To spend that night together. But it wasn't to be. "What would have happened?" she asked. "When you suggested we leave and go find a quiet place?"

"For a long time," he said quietly, "I thought of nothing else. But, like you, this isn't how I thought of our second chance."

Heat flushed through her at his words. Deliberately trying to keep the conversation focused, she said, "I still don't understand what that one man who kidnapped us is all about."

"And that's why a part of me says you need to stay here to be safe, but another part of me says I need you to come back with me, where we can set this up properly and hopefully bring this all to a head."

"Use me as bait?"

He winced, gave a one-arm shrug.

She nodded. "It makes sense. I can't say I like it much. But it makes sense."

"None of this makes sense," he said. "It's so damn stupid."

"Until it does make sense," she said with a smile. "That's the best answer."

"I'll have to set it up," he said, staring at her, watching her expression.

She rose with a nod.

Now that he had her permission, he could get moving on this. "I'll get some extra men and more intel. I've requested more information regarding Rob's time in Thailand, as well as his military record, to see just what's going on. I'm on it," he said, waggling his phone. "Are you sure? No kiss?"

She smiled, leaned up, kissed him gently on the cheek, and said, "Not until it's over."

"Why is that?" he whispered as she drifted past.

"Because, when we start," she said, staring him directly in the face, "this time we won't quit." And she turned and headed for the door.

"OR YOU COULD stay the night," Lennox said, his voice

husky and deep. He watched as she froze at the doorway. He wasn't sure if she was considering it or was just shocked.

Slowly, ever-so-slowly, she turned to face him. "Seriously?"

Uncomfortable, awkward, and certainly not the way he expected this to go down, he refused to lie. "Yes," he whispered. "Why not?"

"*Why not?*" she asked, her tone cutting.

He winced. "That's not what I meant. But I don't want to wait," he said. And that was a shit response too. Women liked to be wooed, and that's the last thing he was doing here.

She looked at him carefully. "It might distract you from all this." And she waved her hand, as if he was supposed to understand what *this* was.

"Or it'll laser-focus me on keeping you safe," he said. Then he smiled and whispered, "You know we're heading there." He shut the door behind her, locking it too.

"Yes, I know we're heading here," she murmured, "but I was thinking we'd take more time. Have more romance. A bed where we could relax and spend some time and have coffee in the next morning type of a thing."

"So next time," he said.

He saw her thinking it over and almost immediately discarding it. He reached out, lifted her chin, and said, "I want you," he whispered, and he kissed her gently. "But more than that, I've wanted you these five years that we've been apart." And he kissed her again.

When she could, she whispered, "Me too, but that doesn't mean this is the best time or place."

"I think it does," he said in all seriousness, slowly pulling her toward him until she was flush against him, from hip to chest. "Just think about it," he said. "You won't have to worry about this, our first time together, in the future. You won't have to anticipate or wonder or be scared or wake up with nightmares or anything along that line."

She started to frown, but he lowered his head and kissed the curve of her lips. "No objections?"

Her eyes popped open at that. And she glared at him. He smiled, lowered his head again, and kissed her deeply. She murmured when he lifted his lips. "You can't drug me into this."

"*Drug you?*"

The corner of her lips tilted up. "Seduce me."

"Actually," he said, "I think you were the one doing the seducing." He slid his hands over her shoulders up the back of her neck to sweep across her scalp, his fingers sliding through her hair.

She tried to shake her head gently. But she couldn't move for his hands.

He smiled and whispered, "Yes, you were inciting the flames. You know that," he said, dropping a kiss at the corner of her mouth and then again on the other side. "And you're right. Once we start, we'll never stop."

"So how will that work in our favor tonight?" she asked thickly.

"Maybe it won't," he whispered. "But maybe, just maybe, getting you a little bit out of my head will help me to focus." And he smiled down into that passion-clouded gaze of hers and whispered, "You're all I think about," he said. "That kiss. It was …"

And she whispered her answer at the same time. "… some kiss."

"I know," he whispered, his breath mingling with hers as

he slid his tongue inside, stroking, mimicking the act to follow. His hand slid down her back to her buttocks to cup and to pull her tight against his hips so that she could feel his erection. He shuttered his eyes closed, as it seemed she softened and wrapped even more around him. "You know we want this," he said.

"That doesn't mean we should do this."

"Is it just *this*, you mean?" he asked, but he didn't get an answer. He could feel her waiting. He smiled, his lips kicking up in the corners again. "Do you think I've forgotten you because that kiss we shared was just a moment of lust? You're the first person I think of when I wake up in the morning. You're the last person I think of before I go to sleep at night." He stared down at her, cuddling her close. "You know perfectly well how I feel."

Her eyes widened, and he reached up to place a finger against her lips as she started her protest.

"No. Stop. Remember who walked away on your wedding?" he asked. "Remember who was there when you got to the divorce court? When you were screaming for joy that it was over? Remember who was there to help you out when you got into trouble?"

"That was Carolina," she argued.

"Well, Carolina was there too," he whispered, his heated breath draping over her cheeks and her eyes and her ears. "Because I was. I was there for you."

CHAPTER 14

HELENA COULDN'T BELIEVE what he was saying, but it's what she had so badly wanted to hear. Had dreamed and fantasized about it, and to think that they were here now? Still that niggling sensation said it wasn't the right time. That they should push it off, and then she thought about the five years they'd already pushed off, and she slid her arms up his chest and around his neck and whispered, "Maybe you should"—then she kissed him on the chin, dropping a little tiny trail down his neck—"show me."

And suddenly she was lifted into the air, cradled against his chest, as he walked a few steps to the bunk. He gently lowered her on the mattress. She opened her arms. He shrugged and shook his head. "Too many clothes."

Her heart skimmed against her chest, constricting her breath even further, as he pulled the T-shirt over his head and quickly unbuckled his jeans, kicking off his boots and socks, and stepping out of his pants along with his briefs in the same motion. He was truly gorgeous. A well-built male in his prime and completely unselfconscious about it. She gave a happy sigh. Her body rippled with heat as she noted that his heavily muscled and otherwise incredible male form in truth matched up to the dreams that she'd had of him.

She tried to swing off the bunk, but he wouldn't let her. He sat down beside her, completely unconcerned about being naked, and pulled off her camisole. Next he slid her boy shorts underneath her butt and down, taking her panties with them. When the thin strip of hair showed up, he stopped, his breath catching in the back of his throat as a shudder wrapped itself around and down so visibly she could feel it herself.

When his hands slid under her plump breasts, he whispered, "My God, you're so beautiful."

She smiled, shook her head, and said, "No," she said, "not really. I'm fit. I'm slim, but I'm average."

His gaze heated up as he did one long, full, slow sweep of her body and said, "Sweetheart, I hate to tell you, but, for all that brainpower up there"—and he gently tapped her temple—"you have no clue just how devastating you are."

He lay down beside her, as if afraid to touch her, and just feasted his eyes. Embarrassed, she went to cover her breasts, and he immediately reached out to stop her. He leaned over a nipple, gently laving it with his tongue before taking it into his mouth and sucking deeply.

She moaned as her belly pulsed in response. She just knew Lennox would be slow and thorough. No way this would be a fast coupling. And, sure enough, he moved to thoroughly kiss the entire breast and to slide to the valley between them and to repeat his ministrations on the second one. She was already mindless jelly by the time he worked his way up to her collarbone, and then to her shoulders and under her neck, on to her chin, but he kept avoiding giving her the passionate kisses that she was so desperate to have. She tried to tug him toward her, but he resisted.

"We have all night," he whispered, "and I've waited too long to make this a rush job."

"Well, you can make it a rush job the first time," she

protested with a tiny smile. "The second time, we could take it slow."

"We'll take it slow the second time as well," he vowed.

And she groaned as his hands slid down her arms to gently stroke her fingers, her palms, and then back up the underside to glide along her rib cage as he plumped her breasts once again for feasting.

And then he slowly moved down her body.

She groaned and cried out, twisting as he gave her navel the same amount of care and intention as her breasts and then down to one hip bone, where he took tiny little nibbles.

She groaned. "I can't hold off."

"And why would you?" he asked, as he shifted enough to stroke the outside of her thigh to her feet where he picked up one foot and gently kissed her big toe before taking it in his mouth and suckled.

She groaned and then laughed and then groaned again as her body rippled in need, overwhelmed with awareness of every move he made. Every nerve ending was on fire. When he moved his hands up the inside of her thigh, she shifted her legs wide to give him access.

He gently stroked her curls and then slid one finger deep inside.

She gasped, her hips rising off the bed as he lowered his hand to find the tiny nub.

Without any warning, fireworks exploded in her belly, shooting outward. She cried out, shuddering in his hands.

He dropped kisses up her belly to her ribs and up under her chin before he shifted over her, holding his weight on his elbows as he lowered his head and finally kissed her full on the lips with mind-drugging passion.

She shifted her hips ever-so-slightly, sliding her heels up

the back of his calves and behind his knees, to wrap tightly around his hips. "More, I want more," she whispered. "Show me how you care."

And, with those words, he slipped inside her body.

She arched slowly up against him, pressing her breasts up against his muscular chest, as he seated himself deep within her.

She moaned, as her body stretched, easing at his complete possession.

He lowered his head and groaned, whispering, "I love you," he said ever-so-gently. "I think I always have."

And he ground his hips tight against hers and then slowly withdrew, only to drive in again. Shocked by his words, overwhelmed by her emotions, she could feel yet another orgasm rippling through her by his words alone. He wrapped her tight and drove both of them toward the cliff yet again.

Her heart was so damn full. Yet she realized she hadn't shared anything with him. She slid her arms up as he drove harder, deeper, faster. His eyes closed as he headed for his release. She reached up, snagged him by the ears, and whispered, "Look at me."

He stared down at her, not missing a stroke. His hot gaze focused on her. She realized the love in the gaze she recognized so damn well but had always thought it was something else. But, no, every time he looked at her, it had been with the same intensity.

She smiled. Her finger stroked across his lips as she whispered, "And I, I love you too."

He cried out as his body exploded with his climax.

And, just like that, his enjoyment sent her rolling back off the cliff yet again too. After that, she closed her eyes and dozed off. With she woke again, she was wrapped up in his arms.

He whispered, "Sleep."

She rolled over again, tucking up close, her legs entwined with his, and slept again. When she woke for the third time, he was coming out of the bathroom to join her. She looked up at him. "What time is it?"

"It's five," he whispered. "Go back to sleep."

And she was just too tired to argue. When she woke up the next time, she was alone. She sat up, looked around, winced from the unaccustomed soreness from her night of heavy lovemaking, slipped out of bed, and quickly put on her clothing. As she opened the door, she peered down the hallway, but she saw no signs of anyone. Grateful for that, she slipped across to her room and crawled into her bunk.

"If you think you can hide from me," Carolina said, with a chuckle in her voice, "you're wrong."

"Oh, God!" Helena said. "I was hoping you were still asleep."

"No, woke up in the night anyway," she said, "and I knew where you were."

"Are you mad?"

"If you were with anybody but my brother," she said, "I might be a little miffed, but I could never be mad at you."

"Well, I was with your brother," she said with a happy sigh, as she curled atop the covers and rolled over to face the wall. She didn't want to join the world. She just wanted to exist in her happy glow for a while longer.

"So why did you leave so fast?"

"Because he left," she said. "I didn't want to wake up and have somebody else come in."

"Ah," Carolina said. "Well, you might want to grab your shower now."

"Is that an option?"

"It sure is."

With that, Helena hopped up and headed into the bathroom, where she quickly stripped down and had a shower. She redressed in her same clothes from yesterday and brushed her hair, now freshly shampooed and towel dried as much as she could and then put it in a braid. "Well," Helena said. "Hopefully, this is okay." She stepped out of the bathroom.

Carolina asked, "Why wouldn't it be?"

"I don't know," she said. "I told him to use me as bait." And she explained some of what had happened with Lennox and first Stefano, then later with Rob, all at her apartment. "This Stefano guy seems to think that Lennox is the one who raped the girl in Thailand."

"And, of course, it was Rob."

"But, of course, Rob said that he was innocent. Somehow gave whatever proof that Stefano needed to seem to believe it was Lennox. Setting up Lennox at the same time. And I wonder if his whole thing about setting Lennox up wasn't to get to us," Helena said.

"Yeah, what's this about being completely smitten with you?"

"I don't see it," she said. "I think he just said that to throw Lennox off the trail. Likely drove him nuts at the same time."

"And maybe that's true," Carolina said, "but why?"

"All I think it is, is because he wanted me and possibly you at the same time back then," Helena said. "But I think it became more about destroying Lennox. To have him worry about what this known rapist would do to us."

"And, of course, the worst thought would be that he

brutalizes and rapes us and has our history repeating itself, but with the added edge of a rapist known to Lennox being in control of us, the two most important women in Lennox's life."

"Exactly. When you think about it, Rob's already sicced somebody very dangerous on Lennox. That Stefano guy. That's a lot of hate."

"Or Rob's just lost in that crazy mind of his, and he does think you're his girlfriend."

"I don't think so," Helena said. "I think, once we get to the truth of it, it'll be all about Stefano, the guy who's trying to take out Lennox. Just way too much about his revenge is at work here. I don't see this as a fatal attraction at all."

"That's because you don't see yourself," Carolina said. "You've always referred to me as gorgeous and beautiful, a China doll, and how stunning I was. And yet, for all the beauty and the brains that you have, you've never really understood just how gorgeous you are." Carolina's words were a reminder of what Lennox had said during the night.

Helena had to stop and wonder. "I don't feel beautiful," she said, "and, therefore, in my mind, I'm not beautiful."

"I understand that," she said, "but we can't let our exes make us into what they wanted us to be. Which were sluts in bed and ugly slaves the rest of the time."

"Isn't that the truth?" Helena said sadly. "I still don't see that I have any kind of beauty that would cause this kind of attraction."

"Well, you keep your theory, and I'll keep my mind open," she said. "But I still don't like the idea of you being bait."

"I don't know how it can work out any other way," Helena said. "While we're safe, the guys are chasing around after

Stefano and Rob in the city but getting nowhere. Sure, we know about facial-recognition software, traffic cameras, *blah, blah, blah,* but the bad guys are always a couple steps ahead of our good guys. I'm sure by now, our guys have tracked down the history of Rob's apartment in my building. They'll find out he never lived there, that he deliberately placed himself in those cameras. Misdirection or a decoy or whatever the reason. The apartment probably isn't even his. Maybe he just subleased it off some guy. Or he's living there without anyone knowing."

"Just to set the scene that you're dating him?"

"Yes," Helena said. "What bothers me more is this other guy, Stefano. How has he tracked us, and how is he so in the know as to what's going on with us? Then again, it's possible he had access to military intel himself. All these guys have connections," She sighed. "That was one of the things that worried Lennox."

"I would think so," Carolina said. "So, how well do you know Sasha and John?"

Helena walked toward Carolina with a frown and sat on the bottom bunk. "Are you serious?"

Carolina rolled over and propped herself up on one elbow. "Well, think about it. They've been with us for the last couple years that we've been doing Red Cross trips. And they happened to be on the same flight to Munich, letting everybody know where we were."

"They went home. We went a different way."

"But we still said we were going home, not necessarily where *home* was but back to the US."

She thought about it and nodded. "I guess it's possible," Helena said. She looked down at Carolina and her phone in her bag. "And I never even thought about it, but what are the chances that we're being tracked even now?"

"I don't know why they would have gone to the apartment, if that were the case. They would have tracked us to the safe house and then here, right?"

"True," Helena said. "I don't know. It's too damn confusing."

Just then a knock came on the door.

As Helena was closer, she walked over and opened it. Lennox stepped in, wrapped her up in a hug without giving her a chance to stop him, and kissed her thoroughly. As Carolina chuckled behind them, he finally lifted his head and said to Helena, "Good morning."

"Good morning," Helena said when she could finally speak. "Did you have to do that?"

Gavin stood behind Lennox, grinning.

"Absolutely," Lennox said. "This way, nobody is under any illusions about our relationship."

"And I didn't mean that," she said drily. "I meant, did you have to scramble my brains so early in the morning?"

And, at that, the rest of the room broke out laughing.

He grinned at her, leaned down, gave her another gentle kiss, and said, "How about the coffee?" he said. "As I recall, you're grumpy without enough coffee in you."

"Is she ever," Carolina said, hopping off the top bunk. "Come on. Let's get food too and set up a game plan. I really don't like the idea of you using her as bait."

"But I do," Helena said. "It's the only answer that makes any sense."

"It does make sense," Gavin said, "but I'm not a big fan of it either."

"And I also think," Helena continued, "that whole relationship spiel by Rob is BS. I think it's to throw you off your game. If he grabs me and potentially Carolina, it's to make us suffer as the Thai girl suffered. Just to get back at you."

At that, Lennox stopped and stared down at her.

She nodded. "Because he knows that, when you find out, you'll hit the red zone really fast and go after him."

"You're right," Lennox said in a suspiciously quiet voice. "I'm going to kill him."

And, at that, he turned and walked away.

LENNOX DIDN'T WANT to leave her to wake up alone, but he had had no choice. When he was called upstairs by Gavin, they had a lot of information coming in, and the biggest and most important was that both Stefano and Rob were still hanging around Helena's apartment area. They were quickly managing to stay ahead of cameras but had been spotted by a couple police cruisers. That chase had led them nowhere but was enough confirmation for Lennox to know that the two bad guys were in that area.

Now, as the group was seated at the table in the ship, and ended up with coffee and then food, Lennox smiled his thanks to the men who had delivered it all and said, "We'll be out of your hair soon."

"Too bad," one of the men said. "Helena and Carolina have been great to have on board."

"Good," he said. "I'm glad we're not putting you guys out."

The men just smiled and then walked away.

Lennox looked over at Helena. "More conquests?"

"Hardly," she said with a laugh.

"We'll see," he said. Lennox had a rough plan in his

mind, but he still needed to flesh it out. His phone buzzed. It was Keane. He handed over his phone to Gavin to read the text message.

He skimmed it and nodded.

"And what's that mean?" Helena asked.

"It's set up," Lennox said. "We're heading back to your apartment."

"I'm coming too," Carolina said.

He frowned at her, already shaking his head with veto power.

"No way I'm letting you take her into danger if I'm not there."

"Why? So you can be in danger too?" he said in exasperation. "You can stay here where you're safe."

"Ha!" Carolina said. "If she's going, I'm going."

"Not happening," Lennox said, his voice inflexible, at least he hoped so. "I have to look after too many things," he said. "My attention will be divided, and that'll put Helena and you and me and Gavin in danger."

She just glared at him. "What is it that you expect me to do then? Sit here and wait?"

"Well, that'd be nice if you would," he said, his voice serious as he stared at his sister intently.

"There are times to stick up for your sister," Carolina said.

"And there are times when you'll be in the way," Lennox parried.

At that, Helena grabbed Carolina's hand and said, "It's all right. I'll be fine. I'm sure Lennox and Gavin have backup lined up to be there too. Right?" Her gaze went from Gavin to Lennox.

"We have city police, and another unit from Coronado

will be there," Lennox said.

"Perfect!" She looked at Carolina. "Sit here and entertain these men while I'm gone," she joked. "It was on me last time. It'll be you this time."

Carolina looked at her, rolled her eyes, and said, "That's hardly fair. I get to be the entertainment while you get to be the main course."

Helena wrinkled her face up at that phrase. "That's not really a nice way to look at this."

Unfortunately, as far as Lennox was concerned, that was a little bit too real. As soon as they were done eating, he said, "We need to go."

She immediately stood and said, "I'm ready. So, is Carolina just sitting here with our gear?"

Lennox nodded. "We thought about taking her onshore, but we just can't take any chances of somebody snagging her too. She's safe here."

"Fine," Carolina said in a dark tone. "But you owe me."

He chuckled and hugged her, kissing his sister on the cheek. "Stay safe."

And, with that, he led the way down, where they disembarked on a small Zodiac that would take them to shore. Once they got back on the dock, they walked along the pier.

As they headed to the main parking lot, she asked, "Do you guys have wheels? And don't tell me that we're traveling in that neon-green Jeep."

"The Jeep is what we want right now," Gavin said. "We want to be seen."

She stayed quiet at that. "Okay," she said, "and I did eat, and I did have coffee, so I guess let's go and get this started."

Lennox looked at her, smiled, and kissed her gently. "It will be fine. I'll make sure nothing happens to you."

She rolled her eyes at him. "I have to trust that, if you came halfway across the world to save us, you'd keep me safe on home ground."

"Absolutely," he said. "Besides, now I've got an awful lot more reasons to keep you safe."

She flushed bright red as his laughter rolled through the Jeep. She shook her head and muttered, "Men." She stared out at the city around them.

He grinned. Life was pretty damn good right now. And it needed to stay damn good. Then the smile fell off his face. He would be pretty damn pissed if either of those men took away what he had waited five years for.

No way in hell he would let that happen.

CHAPTER 15

WITH LENNOX BESIDE her, she hopped out of the Jeep and looked up at her apartment. "You know something? For a long time," she said, "it looked like I would never come back here."

"I'm surprised you didn't rent it out," Lennox said.

"I didn't need the money," she said. "I always wanted to have it available, even for our breaks, even when we were going to Munich."

"That's what I mean. I thought you would have rented it," he said.

She shrugged. "I'm thinking about selling it."

"And buying something else or just not having a home base?"

"That was the problem. I did have a home base," she said, "but I never returned to it. The last two years I've only been here not even a handful of times."

"Well, you've been pretty busy traveling around the world."

"Yep," she said, yawning, "but that's coming to an end now too. So maybe I will be back here more often."

"More often or all the time?" he asked. He wrapped an arm around her shoulder and walked her toward the apartment building. She looked around but saw no sign of Gavin. She glanced up at Lennox sideways. "I presume eyes are on us?"

"Lots of them."

"It's a little too obvious, isn't it?"

"Isn't what too obvious?" he asked.

"Well, surely Rob and Stefano will be expecting surveillance."

"Yep, they will," he said, "which is why we have to be a little tricky."

She entered the security code, walked into the building as the door opened, and looked around. It felt foreign, yet familiar. "It doesn't feel like home anymore," she said abruptly.

"Particularly after all this mess," he said.

They took the stairs up to her second-floor apartment. As she walked down the hallway, she looked around and said, "I don't know any of the neighbors. I don't know anybody who even lives in the building."

"You haven't been here enough to make friends," he said. "You have to actually live in a place to meet your neighbors."

"Right." At her door, she looked at it and said, "I may not have my key with me." But she went through her purse, pulled out her wallet, and found her key. She popped it in and unlocked the door, and, as soon as it was open, Lennox stepped forward and entered first. With her following close behind, he walked in.

Helena put her purse down on the table and stared around that room. It was the refuge she'd built for herself after she had left her husband. For a retreat, nothing was friendly or cozy about it. Then she hadn't lived here enough to make it hers either. She needed a place stay, and this had been it. But, because the apartment wasn't home, she'd been more than happy to leave it behind. She shook her head at the vagaries of human nature and walked into her bedroom. As she opened up the closets, she found clothes that she'd forgotten about. She smiled as she pulled out several outfits and laid them on the bed.

"What are you doing?" Lennox asked.

She stopped, frowned, and then shrugged. "I guess I was picking up more clothes."

"Interesting," he said, but his voice turned to almost a growl, and he crossed his arms over his chest.

She looked up at him and frowned. "Why not? It doesn't feel like home," she said with a shrug. "I think I'd rather go to a hotel."

"Interesting," he said again, "because of Rob and Stefano both being in here?"

"Maybe," she said, "but you know what? The furniture I bought at a secondhand store, so it's not even what I wanted. I just needed a base after the divorce."

"Do you associate this place with the divorce?"

"I don't think so," she said slowly. "I don't know."

"But neither do you want to stay here, considering you're already packing up more clothes?"

She couldn't help herself from agreeing with that, as she walked back to her closet and pulled out a large suitcase. "I feel like I'm packing to leave," she said, "and I know I haven't really decided that, but it's what I feel like I need to do."

And she opened up the large suitcase, found a smaller one inside, and opened it up too. She proceeded to go through the clothing in her closet. Almost nothing was here. She'd taken a significant amount with her but, over time, had gotten rid of the excess and had only kept a few outfits because she wore scrubs most of the time. She packed up what there was, then went to the dresser, and sorted all that. And it still just barely filled the one suitcase. She looked around and said, "The place looks so sterile."

"Again because you haven't lived here."

"True," she said. "I don't want to live here either."

"And where do you want to live?" he asked, his tone curious, as if he wondered what she was doing.

She turned, looked at him, planted her hands on her hips, and asked, "Honestly?"

He nodded. "Yes, that's why I asked."

"With you." There, she'd said it. He had opened his heart up to her last night, and she hadn't had a chance to do very much in return. But, right now, in this cold empty apartment, it's how she felt.

He looked at her in surprise.

She raised both hands, then planted her fists on her hips. "And yet you don't say anything."

"Well, I'm a little stunned," he said slowly, as he walked toward her. His hands stretched out, reaching for hers.

"Well, you shouldn't be," she said crossly. "It's one of the reasons why I wanted to wait until this nightmare scenario was over."

"And I didn't want to wait," he said, tugging her into his arms. "And you're right. We've been heading for this moment for a long time, and there's no need for us to live apart."

She tilted her head back. "But I don't think we're ready for a commitment, like moving in together."

"I don't know about you," he said calmly, "but I am. And obviously you're not committed to staying here."

She looked around and said, "I feel like I've already removed the little bit that was me."

"I think so too. What about the bathroom? Do you have more in there? Because, when we leave today, we can leave permanently. We can get a company in to move all your furniture out. If you don't want any of it, maybe it can go to charity, or you can sell it."

"Not a bad idea," she said, brightening. "But," she said, turning to look back at him, "is it okay to move in with you? Do you live on base? Have you got a place of your own? What's going on in your life?"

And he laughed. "It's a good time to ask," he said, smiling at her. "I am in a new job, as you know," he stated. "I am still with the government, but it's black ops, so you won't ever hear too much information about the type of work I do. Sometimes I'll be home. Sometimes I'll be gone, but I have a home here."

"Good, I'll likely be gone too," she said. "A house or a townhome or what?"

He smiled, leaned over to kiss her nose, and said, "You'll find out."

She shrugged. "I'm good with that. I prefer a house over an apartment any day though." In the bathroom was a bottle of shampoo and conditioner and a couple creams, her toothpaste, and a pack of unopened toothbrushes. "Like I said, sterile." And she quickly packed up the little bits and pieces with the one suitcase still not quite full and the second one empty. She walked into the kitchen. "Maybe there's a coffeemaker," she said. "I think I have all that kind of stuff here."

He went ahead and opened up a few cupboards. "I see a few canned goods and a couple appliances," he said, "but not a whole lot else."

"And they're almost brand-new," she said. "Honestly I think some are still in the closet."

"What are?"

"The boxes that came with the appliances," she said. She walked over to the front closet. And she pulled it open, and there was the coffeemaker box and a toaster box and a coffee grinder box. He just laughed, grabbed them, and said, "Well, let's pack the appliances up in these too," he said. "You never know when you'll need a spare."

"Maybe we should make some coffee first," she said, and she quickly put on a pot. As she looked at him, she said, "How long do we wait?"

"We're here until …" he said, and he didn't finish his sentence.

"Fine," she said. "That works." She had to avoid thinking about it. "We'll need lunch though."

He opened the fridge, but it was 100 percent empty, except for a box of baking soda. "There's not even ketchup or mustard packets here."

She shrugged. "Not exactly my thing."

"We can always order in."

"Or maybe we can walk down and pick up something too. After all, somebody has to have an opportunity to come in and grab me."

He just raised an eyebrow and shrugged.

She realized he already had plans but wasn't sharing them. She went through the kitchen cupboards and found a set of pots and some cutlery, but 90 percent of the cabinets were empty. This packing up activity pushed up bits and pieces in her memory. "I remember the last time I was here, about eight months ago," she said. "I was thinking how my home kitchen was like a hotel kitchenette. The basics but nothing personal."

"Did you walk away from your marriage with nothing?"

She shot him a shuttered look. "Mostly," she said. "I wanted nothing as a reminder. He wanted it all."

"I hope you got your fair share."

"I did," she said, "after the lawyers wrangled about it."

"He should have gone to jail."

"And I just wanted to walk away," she said. "Yes, he could have gone to jail, and we could have had a big trial and all the whole nasty mess of it," she said. "But he ended up with the house and all the contents, and I took the bank accounts. I was good with that."

"And then came a stern warning," Lennox said.

She stopped, slowly turned, looked at him, and said, "What stern warning?"

He just looked at her steadily.

"You?"

He shrugged. "How do you think I felt, finding out what he'd done to you for all those years? Years that I had wanted to be with you, and instead you were with him, with an asshole who used to take his temper out on you."

"Carolina's husband was worse than mine," she said slowly. "But I did learn what fear was, and that's something new in my life now."

"I'm so sorry," he said.

"I am too. It took me long enough to realize what was happening, with the verbal abuse—the bullying, the manipulation, the attack on my mind—but, once he really beat me up," she said, "I never went back. Up until then, it was just lots of threats and the odd smack and a grip that was a little too hard and a shove that was a bit too forceful. But, once he lost it, well, believe me, we were done."

"Good," he said. "He won't be beating up any other female either."

"Did you scare him that badly?"

Again he just stared at her.

"Good," she said, her heart light, her voice cheerful. "I hope you punched him a good one for me."

"More than one. Pretty sure I identically bruised his body and inflicted the same damage on him that he inflicted on you."

She thought about that for a long moment, then smiled. "Thank you."

He gave a self-conscious shrug.

"No," she said, walking across the floor, stroking his cheek, before stretching up on her tiptoes to kiss him gently. "I mean, *thank you*. You did what I couldn't do."

He nodded. "Somebody needed to, and, if you wouldn't take him to court, he needed to know that his behavior wasn't acceptable and that he couldn't go around beating up women."

"He's one of those scaredy-cats. So, if you scared him right, he'll never touch another woman again," she said with a big grin.

Crack!

LENNOX THREW HELENA to the floor, her head coming down hard, only to land in his hand. She looked up at him in shock.

"Stay down," he said hoarsely. He raced to the living room window. Glass had shattered into the apartment. Standing where he was, he peered through the curtains, his phone out as he contacted Gavin. "Sniper's in the apartment building across from us," he said.

"We've got two cops over there," Gavin said.

"Well, somebody may have taken them out." He watched and saw a glint of light and said, "He's at the corner apartment."

"Yeah, that's not where the cops are," Gavin said. "I'll contact them to make sure they are okay. Are either of you hurt?"

"No," Lennox said. "Now the question is, *Who's the shooter?* Rob or this Stefano guy?" He turned to check on Helena. She curled around the kitchen counter, staring at him. "The shooter was on the apartment balcony across the street."

She nodded. "My first guess is Stefano. But then I doubt he'd miss. So maybe Rob?" She shrugged. "So, now what?"

"Well, it's a good thing you didn't want to stay here," he said. "Make sure you keep your shoes on."

"Is it safe to clean up the glass?"

"Not until we get the word that nobody is out there looking to take a second shot."

"And do you think they'll come here and check to see if they succeeded?"

"Somebody should," he said. "Why don't you take a cup of coffee and maybe just stay in your bedroom?"

"I can do that," she said. She walked over to the coffee-maker, quickly poured herself a cup of coffee, and headed back into the bedroom. She finished packing, even securing the smaller folding suitcase inside the larger one. She put it close to her bedroom door. That would go with her. She sat on her bed, intent on getting anything she really wanted during this trip. This visit would be her last one here. There was the bedding to pack up too.

She remembered she had a few moving boxes in the storage room too. She could use those to pack up the rest of her kitchen.

As she sat here, she realized that, if necessary, in an hour she could be completely packed up, and everything moved out. Such a bizarre feeling. She'd put a lot of time and effort into setting up her first marital home. That had been a complete wash by the end of two years of marriage. But she was okay with the mistake she'd made. She just didn't plan on making more like it. As she waited for Lennox to join her, a shadow fell across her bedroom doorway, and she still jolted.

"It's just me," he said in a calming tone.

"Of course it is," she said, taking a deep breath. She sat, frozen on the bed, and looked up at him. "It's just so weird."

"I know," he said, "but somebody has made a move, and that means people are jumping on it and trying to track him down."

"But is it the kidnapper or Rob?"

"I don't know," he said. "I'm expecting both to be here."

She smiled, nodded, and said, "I have empty boxes in my storage room downstairs. If we could get a few of those, we can have the entire kitchen and whatever else I've forgotten about all packed up and moved out right away. *Today.* A company can come in and move the few pieces of big furniture." As she looked around, she said, "I only have a dresser, a night table, and a bed in here. A couch and a chair in the living room, and that little kitchen table is folding."

"We can arrange for that later," he said.

"I guess that sniper shot means we can't get to the storage room and get those boxes, huh?"

He frowned, thought about it, and said, "You know that's a bad idea. Still, we can possibly meet our sniper head-on. Leave your suitcase here, grab your purse, and let's go down and take a look."

She frowned. "What are you expecting?"

"I'm not *expecting* anything," he said, "but we need to do something to shake them up."

"As long as you can protect me, I'm good with it," she said.

"Believe it or not, a half-dozen guys are here."

"I believe it," she said. "But I also know what these assholes are like. And I don't think they'll particularly care where they take me out, as long as they do."

"No," he said quietly. "It's not you they're after."

She stopped, frowned, looked at him, and whispered, "That bullet was for you, wasn't it?"

He nodded.

"Well then, I can go down to the storage locker, and you stay here." He just shot her a look, and she shrugged. "Otherwise we wait. Because it's you they're after. They're looking for an opportunity to take you out, and that is something I don't want to happen."

"Doesn't mean you've got a choice in it," he said.

She frowned. "But I should have a choice."

His phone buzzed then. He pulled it out, checked it, and said, "Gavin had one of the Coronado guys check the sniper's location and another to check on the cops in that building. No shooter was found in the apartment building on the far side of the street. The two cops are fine. They didn't see anyone."

"So this guy got into the apartments on the other side of the road, and the cops never saw him?"

"Exactly."

"Okay, so that's not good."

He shrugged.

When a knock came at her front door, she frowned and looked at him.

He said, "Don't answer it."

"But we need to," she said. The knock came again. And she hesitated. "What if I let him in?"

Lennox pulled a handgun from his back waistband and said, "Let me answer it." He walked up to the door and said, "Hello?"

"It's Gavin. Let me in."

Lennox opened the door and stepped back, and Gavin walked in with a couple bags of food.

"Believe it or not, I was just picking up lunch," he said, "when the shooting happened."

"Oh, good," she said. "I was hungry. There's glass everywhere though, so watch where you walk."

Gavin took a look at the glass doors, nodded, carried the bags to the kitchen table, and then looked around. "Are you guys okay? What's going on here?"

"We're packing me up," she announced. "I need the boxes from the storage room though."

He nodded. "I can go down and take a look. Where are they? Where's your storage locker?" Helena gave him instructions and the combination to the lock. "I'll be back in five," Gavin said, and he left again.

She looked at Lennox. "What's that look on your face for?"

He shrugged and walked over to the table.

She loved the smell of noodles. She quickly pulled out the containers, laughing because Gavin brought so much.

"Did he expect to feed the whole apartment building? Only three of us are here."

"Actually," Gavin said, "I thought you'd be hungry."

He was back awfully quick, and he had an odd tone to his voice. Lennox turned and swore. Because Stefano held a gun to Gavin's head.

"Move back," Stefano said, and he stepped in and closed the door behind him.

Lennox stood and stared at him. "So you took that pot shot at me through the living room window just now?"

Stefano nodded.

"I already told you that I had nothing to do with your sister."

Stefano nodded. "So you say. But I want proof."

"What kind of proof?" Lennox asked, swearing at the sudden turn of events.

"You need to tell me what happened to my sister."

At that, the tumblers clicked into place. "I can tell you," Lennox said, "but you won't like it." And he told him how he'd caught Rob with the girl in a hotel room. Lennox and Rob had been in town at the hotel's bar. Lennox rarely drank to the excess, but Rob had been on a weird bender lately, and he wanted to go out and get completely smashed. But halfway through the evening, he disappeared, taking an elevator up into the hotel itself. When Lennox had noticed, he'd gone looking for him, asking the hotel employees for any disturbance reports from the other guests in the hotel, and finally found Rob in a hotel room with a young girl. And he had already beaten her up badly. Lennox stopped him going any further.

"I spoke to my sister," Stefano said. "She says she doesn't know what he looked like, as he had a mask on."

"And it was dark, wasn't it?"

He nodded. "But now," he said, "now I can't tell whether it's you or Rob. Rob is one who told me it was you, and now you tell me it's Rob. I wanted to kill you earlier with my sniper round, but then realized I couldn't without knowing the answers."

"Of course Rob told you it was me," Lennox said, hearing the confirmation from Stefano. "Rob hates me and would do anything to punish me."

"So I have an answer to this problem," the kidnapper answered.

"I'm scared to ask, but what is your answer?"

The kidnapper grinned. "I will kill both of you. Immediately."

CHAPTER 16

HELENA COULDN'T WRAP her mind around the kidnapper's words. "How could you possibly think that Lennox would have anything to do with a rape?" she cried out.

Lennox tried to keep her back and out of the way, but the kidnapper looked at her almost dispassionately. "He hurt my sister," he said. "How can you think I wouldn't want revenge?"

She opened her mouth and then slammed it shut because she knew precisely what Lennox had done to the two men who had beaten up her and his sister. "I understand that," she said quietly, "but what if you have the wrong man?"

He just glared at her, then shrugged. "That's why I must kill them both."

"And did you talk to your sister? Did you ask her for details?"

"How can I possibly do that?" he cried out in frustration. "It's not like I'll have her dredge all that up again. It hurts her."

"Of course it does, and I would hate to even imagine what that would be like," she said. "But I do understand what it's like to be beaten up, and I do understand what it's like to be afraid of a man. What about his voice? Could she say anything about that? Why was she in the hotel?"

His glare grew.

"Was she just traveling? Was she a tourist? What was she doing?"

"She was visiting my brother, who was teaching English there. She woke up to Lennox here in the room with her."

"And how do you know it was Lennox?"

"She said it was Lennox."

"Meaning, the guy *said* his name was Lennox?"

Stefano nodded.

"So a rapist went into a young woman's room, used her badly, left her beaten, and then told her what his name was?"

He stopped, shaking his head. "I don't know how it came out," he said, "but she found out that was his name."

"That's the name he *used*," she said. "That doesn't mean it was his name."

He glared at her silently.

"She didn't say anything about his hair, about the size of his hands, his scars?"

"I didn't ask," he said. "She was adamant. It was Lennox who had beaten her up."

"Okay," she said, "you got your sister's number on your phone?"

"I'm not calling her," he said calmly. "I'll just take them both out, and then I'll know for sure I got the right one."

"And how would your sister feel if you killed a completely innocent man?"

"She won't know."

"Maybe not," Helena said. "Maybe I'll contact her after this and let her know what you did."

Immediately the gun turned in her direction.

"So it's not about revenge," she said. "It's just about being another one of the assholes responsible for getting your sister raped."

Fury lit his face.

She nodded. "You're not here because of what somebody did to your sister. You're here because you couldn't protect your sister."

The shock from her verbal blow was a direct hit.

She nodded again. "I get that," she said, "but, if you were protecting your sister back then, you wouldn't now be looking to face down the man who physically hurt her," she said quietly. "This is not that man."

"So, because you love him, you defend him."

"Of course I love him. And, yes, I defend him," she said. "But I can tell you that he's not the rapist. I spent two years at the hands of a man who beat me up. I know the difference."

And, for the first time, she saw Stefano waver.

"I understand the feeling of violation," she said. "I understand the feeling of betrayal. But I don't understand why you would think it was Lennox, just because the man who raped her says it was Lennox." She nodded, motioning at Stefano's neck. "What do all the scars on your face have to do with this?"

"That's why I know it was Lennox," he said, but his voice lacked conviction.

"What are you talking about?" she asked.

"I was there too, and she called me, screaming, and I chased him down. This is from a bullet," he said, reaching for his cheek. "And the burns are from when he brought a shed down on top of me."

"And what about him? Did he get any injuries from all that?"

He nodded. "I shot him." And he glanced at Lennox.

"Where did you shoot him?" Helena asked quietly, having seen all of Lennox in his beautiful naked glory the night before.

"In his side," he said.

"So then, if I show you Lennox's side, and you see no bullet wound, will you believe that it's not him?"

Again the gun wavered.

She walked over to Lennox and said, "Sorry, sweetie," as she lifted his T-shirt to the middle of his chest. Then she showed Stefano. "No bullet wound. On either side of Lennox."

The man stared at Lennox, stared all along his waist, and then back up at his face. But obviously Stefano was confused. "You're a different shape," he said, but everyone in the room could tell that Stefano was still trying to fit what he wanted to believe into his hypothesis.

"It wasn't Lennox," she said. "And I understand that you're angry and that you're upset and that you desperately want to take down the man who hurt your sister, but it wasn't Lennox."

Stefano gave a harsh sigh and slowly lowered his gun and gave Gavin a hard shove, pushing him farther into the apartment. "Then who was it? Rob?"

"Yes," Lennox said. "Rob raped your sister. I'm the one who turned him into the military police. He went to jail because of me. And now we're after him because he's after my girlfriend," Lennox said quietly.

The kidnapper looked at Helena.

She nodded. "Thanks to you, three others and I were kidnapped and carted off to Poland," she snapped. "Held in a damn cage for a couple days. Terrorized and, at the same time, found out that Rob was the one behind all of it, and he's still trying to kill Lennox to get his hands on me. All as payback to Lennox."

Stefano frowned.

"You've been used," she said. "What I'm trying to say is that, Rob is trying to get you to take out Lennox so that it leaves the field clear for Rob to get me."

"Why would he want that?"

She gave a half laugh. "That's what I keep telling people. I don't know why. I'm not some femme fatale."

Stefano just waved it off. "But why would he want somebody else to do his killing?"

"Because he's not a killer," Lennox said. "When the circumstances demanded that, while we both were in the navy, he would step up to the plate and do it, but he's not a cold-blooded killer, and we were friends once," he said. "We were friends until I took him to court over what he did to your sister."

The man's eyes widened in shock. "You're the one who had him punished? You're the one who sent him to jail?"

He nodded. "Yes, that's why he hates me. That's why he told you and somehow convinced you that I'm the one who hurt your sister. And how did you hear that?"

"In jail," he said. "Our younger brother was there. With him—with Rob, who was unfairly accused. But I never saw Rob's face."

"No, he wasn't *unfairly* accused," Helena said calmly. "He was justly accused."

"And that's why you also said it wasn't me in this apartment earlier," Lennox said, as if finally understanding. "Because you already had a battle with Rob, and you knew his body and where your shot hit him, but you still didn't know his face, but then you couldn't fit my body type in with your memories."

Slowly Stefano nodded. "I don't like being used."

"Do you think your brother had anything to do with it?"

He frowned. "There's a reason my brother was in jail."

"Right," she said, "because he's not trustworthy."

Lennox added, "Maybe he had something to do with this. Maybe Rob paid him?"

Stefano frowned, took a step back, and said, "I must think about this."

"You do that," Lennox said. "And maybe don't point that gun at me or mine again, much less shoot at me. I've given you a couple passes for waving that gun around. But after that shot across the road into this apartment, I won't give you another one."

The two men gazed at each other; their expressions were hard and determined.

Stefano made one clipped nod and disappeared into the hallway. They could hear his footsteps running.

Gavin and Lennox looked at each other. It's almost as if they made a silent joint decision to not go after Stefano.

Helena spun around and said, "He still kidnapped me. Doesn't that count?"

Lennox grabbed her, tucked her up close, and said, "Yes, it counts. And how do you feel about punishing him, now that you have more details?"

And she realized what he was saying because it wasn't just about punishing Stefano for what he was doing. It was about his motivation behind his actions. He had simply wanted justice for his sister.

And that's precisely what Lennox would have done for both his sister and for Helena. And so, in his mind, he was already saying this Stefano guy did not need to be punished. If she didn't agree, he needed to know now because it would be part of the elements that built their ongoing relationship. She sagged against him and said, "Well, he's just damn lucky he didn't hurt any of us."

"I know," he murmured against her hair, holding her close. "What we need to do is find his brother."

"He is, hopefully, still in jail."

"Also," Gavin said, "I managed to get a tracker on Stefano."

Lennox grinned at him. "Perfect audio?"

Gavin held up his phone, which even now crackled as it began to receive. "We've got audio."

"Any chance we can eat now?" Helena asked. They walked to the table, and she could feel exhaustion hitting her. "How do you deal with all this adrenaline?" she asked, as she served herself up food. Just then a voice came over Gavin's phone. She didn't understand the language, but Lennox immediately brought his phone out and recorded it. As soon as the call was finished, he sent the file to somebody. "Are you getting that translated?"

"I am," he said. "An awful lot of yelling and shouting went on there."

"Yeah," she said. "I suspect my kidnapper contacted his brother for clarification."

"Yes," Lennox said. "That would be my take on it too."

She reached for a fork and dug into a large bowl of noodles. "At least we've got food." She beamed at Gavin.

Gavin smiled and said, "You keep your head remarkably well in these situations."

"So do you," she said. "I'm not the one who had a gun at my head."

"Maybe not," he said. "But it was pretty intense. How do you get that kind of experience?"

"Sometimes our circumstances when we're operating overseas are pretty intense too," she said. "I'm a surgeon, and I do very well under pressure."

Gavin studied her for a long moment, then nodded. "You're a good person to have around then."

"Glad to hear it. What's next?" She forked up noodles and chewed as she listened to the men.

"Maybe," he said, "the bottom line is, we make sure that we find Rob. Because, if this Stefano guy finally understands how he's been taken, he'll go after Rob too."

"I'm not against that," Lennox said. "Saves me from doing the job."

"In a way, it's the best of both worlds," Helena said. "Stefano gets his revenge. Rob gets what's due to him. And we get off scot-free."

Lennox looked at her and smiled and said, "You really do have that fairy-tale thing going on, don't you?"

"Absolutely," she said. "Just think about it. The fairy tales are coming true in so many other ways. Why not this one too?"

GAVIN ROLLED HIS eyes.

Lennox chuckled. "Poor Gavin. You'll find yours."

"My what?" he asked. "Revenge?"

"Partner," she said.

"Well, I hope I don't have to wait five years to make a move on her," he said in disgust.

At that, she burst out laughing. "Good point." She

reached for one of the other cartons and said, "You going to finish that?"

Lennox watched as she dug into the food. "Do you always eat this much?"

"Sometimes," she said. "I do like my groceries." And she plowed into a big dish of veggies. As she ate, she looked up at him and said, "Now we can get the boxes from the storage room, and we can finish packing up. What are we expecting to happen from here on in?"

"Rob," Lennox said. "We still need Rob."

"He obviously still has a lot of anger for you."

"I messed up his life."

"No," she said, "*he* messed up his own life. You just made him pay for it."

"Means the same thing to Rob," Lennox said.

She shrugged at that. "So what do we do to bring in Rob?"

"Not sure," Lennox said. "But I don't suspect we'll have to wait long to find out." He got up and piled the empty cartons in the to-go bag and asked, "Where's the outdoor garbage?"

"Down the hallway," she said. "A big bin drops down to the Dumpster in the basement."

"Good," he said. "I'll take this load out, so we don't have to worry about it later. And I'll swing down below and grab the cardboard boxes."

She nodded.

And he stood, he packed up everything that he could for the garbage, then stepped outside, checked that the hallway was empty, and walked toward the chute. He dumped the trash and then opened the stairwell and ran down to the basement floor. He'd already been in her apartment building and had checked out this level earlier and hadn't found anything of any value. Only a whole roomful of locked up chain-link-style lockers. So no walls to hide behind but plenty of junk to do the job.

That meant a ton of places where somebody could hide, but it wouldn't have been the most comfortable of spots, so Rob would have to choose his poison. Plus it didn't make for easy access, unless Rob left one of the storage units unlocked. Still, that would give away his hiding spot pretty easily.

So Rob rented an apartment here as a foil, just to have a hiding spot in his—or someone else's—storage locker? That could work. That could explain where he disappeared to when the cops were after him, when Lennox had trailed him out his own apartment's patio doors.

Lennox walked to the unit that was hers, used the combination lock, and quickly opened it. He wondered at a woman who kept packing boxes. Grabbing up one large bundle, he moved it out and quickly locked up. Nothing else was in here, just the packing boxes. He shook his head and muttered, "She really wasn't planning on staying."

"Maybe not," a man said from the shadows, "but I could have persuaded her to."

Lennox froze. He turned to see Rob, standing in front of him, with a handgun drawn. "Wow," he said. "This is a little repetitive."

"Hardly," Rob said. "I'm surprised you're still alive."

"Why? Because of your buddy?"

Rob shrugged. "Much better to have a very dedicated and motivated killer coming after you," he said. "Chances are you and I would be equal, but that guy looked like he might even have us beat," Rob said with a laugh.

Lennox thought about Stefano. "He's active military.

Just not our country."

"Of course not," Rob said. "Not even sure what country he is. I think his sister was Norwegian."

"But you didn't care, did you?"

He shrugged. "Nope, I was just looking for a good time. Needed to work off a little lust."

"And how is it that you think a good time is beating up that poor girl as badly as you did?"

Rob grinned widely, a wild look in his eyes.

"But that didn't stop you, did it? And it doesn't matter how young she was either," Lennox said. "You still beat her up and raped her."

"I like rough sex," Rob said. "I'm looking forward to playing with Helena."

"So all that talk about wanting Helena for yourself, … what's that about?"

"Well, I do want her for myself," he said, "but I was just trying to throw you off your stride."

"By telling lies and false tales?"

"Sure, why not?" he said. "Besides, it's not that far off," he said. "I've been fascinated with her ever since I saw her the first time. Unfortunately, that night that I met her, she was already in a tight clench with you. Hence the need to work off some lust."

"So you were interested then?"

"Absolutely," he said. "She's dynamite. But she's also definitely yours, and that made me really angry. Because, if I'd just met her earlier, she wouldn't have given a shit about you."

"She doesn't like rough sex," Lennox said. "So that wouldn't work with her." The fact that he was even talking about Helena with this guy made Lennox furious.

"She's gorgeous, and why the hell should you have her?" Rob snapped. "And then, after what you did to me," he continued, "I couldn't think of anything else. I just wanted to make sure she was mine, that you knew it, and that you died knowing it. And I'm the one who'll be banging her forever, not to mention having the occasional punch up," he sneered.

"Over my dead body," Lennox said.

"Exactly," Rob said, with a big smile. "I wouldn't have it any other way."

"Asshole," Lennox said. His gun was in his waistband tucked in the back. But it would be that much harder to get to, considering Rob already pointed his gun on him. Lennox needed a diversion. "Don't you ever have any remorse about how you hurt that poor girl?"

"She's just a woman," Rob said. "I've had lots of them too. That one, in Thailand though, I don't know why, but I just needed to tear her up a bit. Helena needs to get to know me, and she'll adapt to my ways soon enough."

"Helena and I have known each other since we were kids," Lennox said quietly. "She's been my sister's best friend forever."

And that stopped Rob in his tracks. "Really?"

"Yes," he said, "really."

"Oh, well, it doesn't matter," he said. "If you're not around, she'll turn to me."

"She knows what you've done," Lennox said. "She knows that you raped and beat up that girl and turned her brother to try and kill me."

"Well, yeah, but I didn't do it on my own," he said. "His brother was in the same jail."

"And why is that?"

"Because they were over there together at the same time. And his brother was doing drugs. Got picked up and tossed into jail. His sister was raped because the druggie younger brother was supposed to be sharing the same suite with her and wasn't there to protect her, and the older brother was off at a meeting or something. He wasn't there to protect either of them. So the younger brother turned on the charm and the guilt to make older brother believe that it was you who had hurt her. And that, if the older brother didn't finally get in the act and defend the two of them, then their lives were all completely ruined because of *you*, Lennox."

"How could you even do that to some guy? He's out there, fighting for his country." Lennox saw yet another parallel between Stefano and himself. "Doing the right thing. Here he's got a shitty brother who was supposed to be protecting his younger sister, a sister who got beaten up and raped by an asshole, and then you prime up that guy, and you turn him in my direction."

"Right?" Rob said, laughing. "It's perfect."

"Not perfect," another man said from behind Rob.

Rob froze and backed up flat against the storage units, so he could face the new threat. And there was the kidnapper, Stefano. Lennox quickly pulled the gun from the back of his waistband and pointed it at Rob. "Now what will you do, Rob?" he asked. "There's two of us now."

Rob glared at Stefano and asked him, "What's your problem? Lennox is the one who beat up your sister."

"No," Stefano said, his voice heavy. "I spoke with my brother."

"Oh, that lying little weasel," Rob cried out nervously. "You know he's nothing but a drug pusher, right?"

"I know," Stefano said. "And I kept thinking that maybe

he would get better. He'd been teaching English and doing well, then started to slide. That's why my sister was there visiting him. We knew he was struggling again, and we thought having her there would help."

"And yet," Rob said, "she got badly hurt there too because of Lennox here." Rob motioned his gun in Lennox's direction.

But Stefano shook his head. "No," he said. "I talked to Lennox, and then I talked to her. I already realized that it wasn't Lennox when I initially met him in the apartment here. But I had to go back and talk to my brother to make sure."

"How could you know it wasn't him?" Rob said. "He was there. I saw him." And this time, Rob's voice was getting out of control and echoed throughout the locker room.

Lennox knew Gavin would have noticed how long he'd been gone by now too.

"Because I shot him. *You*," Stefano said. "We raced through the streets, and you ended up torching the small shed we were in, and it went up in flames, *then I shot you.*"

Rob shook his head. "Dude, I don't know what you're talking about. It wasn't me. It was Lennox."

"Even though I was badly burned, I know that I hit you with my shot," he said. "I suffered for the burns and for the bullet hole in my cheek," he said. "That's also why we stayed in Thailand for as long as we were, so I could get treated. My brother was then too scared to say anything because he was afraid you would come back after him."

"And again I think you're misguided," Rob said with a light laugh. "That was Lennox, remember? It's all Lennox."

"My brother made it very clear. He overdosed and was saved and was in the hospital recently, since he got out of jail. He's been a much different person."

"When did this happen?" Rob said in a derisive tone. "Your brother is nothing but a drunken user. A junkie."

"Yes, to all of that," he said, "but now he is going home, and we will work to make his recovery happen. This was just a few days ago. After you resurrected this mess. That's why he had an overdose. Because he realized what he'd done."

"He hadn't done anything," Rob said.

"Yes, he did. He directed me to the wrong man. On purpose. And for what? For money? For drugs? Drugs that he then took and overdosed on. He'll turn over a new leaf," Stefano announced, his accent thick, guttural.

"No," Rob said. "He's nothing but a useless man."

"No," Stefano said. "He has time. He is young. He can make a better life."

"Then I should have killed him," Rob snarled.

"Yes," Stefano said, "you should have. And you should have killed me."

"I can do that now," Rob said.

But Stefano immediately cocked his weapon and said, "I don't think so." Instead of killing Rob, he shot once, and Rob's knee exploded, and he went down screaming.

Immediately Lennox turned his gun on Stefano. "He's down," Lennox said. "In our country, we don't shoot men who are down."

"I know," Stefano snarled. "You're weak too." But he held his gun on Lennox as he walked closer to Rob. Then he crouched in front of Rob and said, "I want you to take that gun of yours, and I want you to put it against your own head," he said.

Rob was crying as he shook his head. "You're nuts! You're crazy!"

"No," Stefano said. "I'm not. But now I see clearly. And I know that you are as bad as my brother said. And that you are the one who raped my sister."

"You could fucking ask her."

"I did," Stefano said slowly. "And she confirmed what I already knew. It was not Lennox."

"How the hell could she know that?" Rob asked, moaning, his hand on his knee.

"Because you are not shaped like him."

Lennox realized his massive upper chest in this instance was as good a descriptor as his height and his hair and eye color. Because it confirmed the moment of truth that they all needed here. Lennox walked to Rob and gently took his handgun from him. Lennox reached down and lifted Rob's T-shirt. "Do you see?"

Stefano looked at the scar on Rob's side, from when he shot him, nodded slowly, and said, "Yes, I see." He punched Rob hard with his fist. Stefano stood, looked down at Lennox, and said, "Now what?"

"I'm not sure," Lennox said honestly. "I need to know you're not coming after me again."

"No," he said. "I'm not."

"And Rob?"

"He needs to die," Stefano said calmly.

"Well, he does," Lennox said. "But, if you do that, then it's murder, and that's a whole different story."

"You will protect him even now? After what he's done against you?"

"It's not that as much as our level of honor involved in this," he said quietly. "Rob is a mess. He needs to go to jail for the rest of his life," he said, "but I still need answers."

"What answers could you need?" Rob muttered as he

came around. "There's nothing else to tell you. I hated your fucking guts, and I wanted this guy to kill you. As a plus I would take Helena as mine. And I would beat her up and bash the shit out of her whenever I wanted to. Just for the fun of knowing that you couldn't stop me."

"I get that," Lennox said, as he stared down at Rob. "Which means you'll always be a threat to her."

He laughed and laughed again. "What will you do? Honorable Lennox won't shoot a man who's down," he said. "It's not who you are."

"Maybe this is a good time to make an exception," Lennox said, but he was torn. "How did you keep track of her all this time?"

"Besides Stefano's intel? John," he said. "And Sasha. Individually. I paid them both."

"They were *both* involved?" Lennox had been afraid of that and already had the Mavericks running the financials on those two. Hearing this would hurt both Helena and Carolina, but Lennox would put in a good word to have both of them thrown in some Polish prison, to keep the Red Cross from getting any fallout because of their greed.

"Yes. And you should have heard them rant and rave at me separately when they found themselves kidnapped by this guy."

"Wow," Lennox said. "The Red Cross will really have a fun time cleaning up the rest of their staff, won't they?"

"I thought Sasha and John would both quit after this anyway because they figured they would get found out eventually."

"Yes," Lennox said. "I'll pay them a visit too."

"Of course you will," Rob said. "You might as well just shoot me," he said. "It'll be easier that way."

"No," Lennox said. "I'm not doing the job."

Stefano squatted beside Rob and held out his gun. "You can do the job yourself. None of us want you around anymore."

Rob glared at him, snatched the handgun from Stefano's hand.

Immediately Lennox held his gun to Rob's head.

"I'm not shooting him," Rob said. "But I'll be damned if I go back to a fucking jail again." And he shoved the gun on his jaw and pulled the trigger.

Silence.

Stefano stood, looked down at the body, and said, "It's the best way."

"Only raises another mess of questions," Lennox said, "because of that handgun. *Your* handgun."

"I will leave it behind," he said. He had gloves on, and he held them up and said, "They won't trace it to me."

"Then you better leave," Lennox said quietly, but a hard look was in his eye. "And make sure I don't see your ass ever again," he said, "or it's mine."

Stefano gave him a ghost of a smile. "Enjoy the years with your woman," he said. "And, if you ever see any more assholes like this guy …"

"I'll do the same thing I did last time," Lennox said. "I'll report him to the authorities and will make sure he gets punished for what he did."

Stefano nodded. "It's much better for everyone that Rob's gone." And, with that, Stefano melted into the shadows and disappeared.

EPILOGUE

"**A**RE YOU SURE I can't look now?" Helena complained good-naturedly, her eyes shut.

"No," Gavin said. "You don't get to look at anything right now."

"That's not fair," she said. Gavin had her in the passenger side of his Jeep. They were heading to Lennox's, and Lennox and Carolina were expecting them.

"And we would have been here a long time ago," Gavin said, "but you're the one who wanted to stop and get flowers."

"Of course I did!" she said, as her arms tightened around the big bouquet. "It's my first visit to Lennox's house."

"Hardly a visit," he said. "You're moving in."

"I am," she said, a blissful smile on her face.

Lennox was, indeed, a lucky man, Gavin thought. He didn't know how the hell these two had finally gotten past their differences, but they had, and that's what counted. And now here Gavin was, taking her to Lennox's house, while she took her first step into their future. Gavin pulled up to the front, parked, and said, "Now I'm coming around to your side."

"Okay, okay," but she hopped out impatiently and waited for him to grab her arm. As they got to the sidewalk, he said, "Now you can open your eyes."

She looked up to see the stone-and-cedar Tudor house in front of them for her very first time, one that Gavin had seen many times. "Oh, my goodness," she said, "it's gorgeous."

The door opened, and Lennox stepped out. She cried out, handed off the flowers to Gavin right before she raced forward. Lennox opened his arms, and she dashed into them. Lennox picked her up and swung her around in his arms.

Gavin stood back and smiled up at them. "You two look perfect together," he declared.

"Good," Lennox said. "It's taken Carolina and me a couple days to get everything ready."

Gavin nodded. His phone went off just then. "Hang on. I'll be there in a minute."

"Don't bother," Lennox said. "I can tell you all about it."

He looked at his phone and back at his buddy and asked, "What is it?"

"The next job," Lennox said. "I've got your orders here. I was going to hand them to you before the call came through, but you guys were late."

Gavin laughed. "Am I going alone?"

"No," Lennox said, "you're going with a friend. You just don't know which one."

"And you?"

"I'm running ground crew," Lennox said with a grin. "I get to stay here with my beautiful Helena."

"Okay, that'll be pretty sucky on my part but perfect for you. Do I get to come inside for a bit before I head out?"

"Sorry, bud."

Just then a military vehicle pulled up to the front of the house.

Lennox held out a brown envelope to Gavin and then pointed. "That's your ride."

"What about my gear?"

"It's all waiting for you." Lennox turned Helena around and said, "Say goodbye to Gavin."

She lifted a hand, confusion on her face.

Gavin smiled and said, "I'll be back."

"We'll wait for you," she said.

He shook his head. "Don't bother. I won't be back for days yet. Have a good one." And he hopped into the truck and headed off. He had the brown envelope from Lennox, but that's all he had. He looked at the driver and asked, "What are your orders?"

"I'm taking you to the dock," he said. "A destroyer's waiting for you."

"Any other details?"

"None," he said.

"Fine, let's go." Gavin was headed somewhere; he just didn't know where yet. And maybe that was okay too.

This concludes Book 10 of The Mavericks: Lennox.

Read about Gavin: The Mavericks, Book 11

The Mavericks: Gavin (Book #11)

What happens when the very men—trained to make the hard decisions—come up against the rules and regulations that hold them back from doing what needs to be done? They either stay and work within the constraints given to them or they walk away. Only now, for a select few, they have another option:

The Mavericks. A covert black ops team that steps up and break all the rules … but gets the job done.

Welcome to a new military romance series by *USA Today* best-selling author Dale Mayer. A series where you meet new friends and just might get to meet old ones too in this raw and compelling look at the men who keep us safe every day from the darkness where they operate—and live—in the shadows … until someone special helps them step into the light.

When four members of one family-owned corporation are kidnapped off the streets in Honolulu, Gavin's intel says this is a corporate espionage case … but is it?

There's not much to like about this case. Too many people are involved, … including an old friend of Gavin's. But, as Gavin digs deeper into the motives of the suspect pool, events get uglier, and bodies start to fall.

Rosalina has no idea how she ended up in this nightmare, but all she cares about is her ailing parents who have been separated from her and her sister. Even when she and her sister are freed, Rosalina finds no sign of their mother or father. Trying to rescue them means deciphering friend from foe …

It comes down to the wire as this close family corporation falls apart, revealing the core of darkness inside, … and leaves Gavin and Rosalina struggling to stay safe as enemies work to take out them both.

Find book 11 here!

To find out more visit Dale Mayer's website.

https://geni.us/DMGavinUniversal

Author's Note

Thank you for reading Lennox: The Mavericks, Book 10! If you enjoyed the book, please take a moment and leave a short review.

Dear reader,

I love to hear from readers, and you can contact me at my website: www.dalemayer.com or at my Facebook author page. To be informed of new releases and special offers, sign up for my newsletter or follow me on BookBub. And if you are interested in joining Dale Mayer's Reader Group, here is the Facebook sign up page.
http://geni.us/DaleMayerFBGroup

Cheers,
Dale Mayer

About the Author

Dale Mayer is a *USA Today* best-selling author, best known for her SEALs military romances, her Psychic Visions series, and her Lovely Lethal Garden cozy series. Her contemporary romances are raw and full of passion and emotion (Broken But ... Mending, Hathaway House series). Her thrillers will keep you guessing (Kate Morgan, By Death series), and her romantic comedies will keep you giggling (*It's a Dog's Life*, a stand-alone novella; and the Broken Protocols series, starring Charming Marvin, the cat).

Dale honors the stories that come to her—and some of them are crazy, break all the rules and cross multiple genres!

To go with her fiction, she also writes nonfiction in many different fields, with books available on résumé writing, companion gardening, and the US mortgage system. All her books are available in print and ebook format.

Connect with Dale Mayer Online

Dale's Website – www.dalemayer.com
Twitter – @DaleMayer
Facebook Page – geni.us/DaleMayerFBFanPage
Facebook Group – geni.us/DaleMayerFBGroup
BookBub – geni.us/DaleMayerBookbub
Instagram – geni.us/DaleMayerInstagram
Goodreads – geni.us/DaleMayerGoodreads
Newsletter – geni.us/DaleNews

Also by Dale Mayer

Published Adult Books:

Hathaway House
Aaron, Book 1
Brock, Book 2
Cole, Book 3
Denton, Book 4
Elliot, Book 5
Finn, Book 6
Gregory, Book 7
Heath, Book 8
Iain, Book 9

The K9 Files
Ethan, Book 1
Pierce, Book 2
Zane, Book 3
Blaze, Book 4
Lucas, Book 5
Parker, Book 6
Carter, Book 7

Lovely Lethal Gardens
Arsenic in the Azaleas, Book 1
Bones in the Begonias, Book 2
Corpse in the Carnations, Book 3
Daggers in the Dahlias, Book 4

Evidence in the Echinacea, Book 5
Footprints in the Ferns, Book 6
Gun in the Gardenias, Book 7
Handcuffs in the Heather, Book 8
Ice Pick in the Ivy, Book 9

Psychic Vision Series
Tuesday's Child
Hide 'n Go Seek
Maddy's Floor
Garden of Sorrow
Knock Knock…
Rare Find
Eyes to the Soul
Now You See Her
Shattered
Into the Abyss
Seeds of Malice
Eye of the Falcon
Itsy-Bitsy Spider
Unmasked
Deep Beneath
From the Ashes
Stroke of Death
Psychic Visions Books 1–3
Psychic Visions Books 4–6
Psychic Visions Books 7–9

By Death Series
Touched by Death
Haunted by Death
Chilled by Death
By Death Books 1–3

Broken Protocols – Romantic Comedy Series
Cat's Meow
Cat's Pajamas
Cat's Cradle
Cat's Claus
Broken Protocols 1-4

Broken and… Mending
Skin
Scars
Scales (of Justice)
Broken but… Mending 1-3

Glory
Genesis
Tori
Celeste
Glory Trilogy

Biker Blues
Morgan: Biker Blues, Volume 1
Cash: Biker Blues, Volume 2

SEALs of Honor
Mason: SEALs of Honor, Book 1
Hawk: SEALs of Honor, Book 2
Dane: SEALs of Honor, Book 3
Swede: SEALs of Honor, Book 4
Shadow: SEALs of Honor, Book 5
Cooper: SEALs of Honor, Book 6
Markus: SEALs of Honor, Book 7
Evan: SEALs of Honor, Book 8
Mason's Wish: SEALs of Honor, Book 9

Chase: SEALs of Honor, Book 10
Brett: SEALs of Honor, Book 11
Devlin: SEALs of Honor, Book 12
Easton: SEALs of Honor, Book 13
Ryder: SEALs of Honor, Book 14
Macklin: SEALs of Honor, Book 15
Corey: SEALs of Honor, Book 16
Warrick: SEALs of Honor, Book 17
Tanner: SEALs of Honor, Book 18
Jackson: SEALs of Honor, Book 19
Kanen: SEALs of Honor, Book 20
Nelson: SEALs of Honor, Book 21
Taylor: SEALs of Honor, Book 22
Colton: SEALs of Honor, Book 23
SEALs of Honor, Books 1–3
SEALs of Honor, Books 4–6
SEALs of Honor, Books 7–10
SEALs of Honor, Books 11–13
SEALs of Honor, Books 14–16
SEALs of Honor, Books 17–19

Heroes for Hire

Levi's Legend: Heroes for Hire, Book 1
Stone's Surrender: Heroes for Hire, Book 2
Merk's Mistake: Heroes for Hire, Book 3
Rhodes's Reward: Heroes for Hire, Book 4
Flynn's Firecracker: Heroes for Hire, Book 5
Logan's Light: Heroes for Hire, Book 6
Harrison's Heart: Heroes for Hire, Book 7
Saul's Sweetheart: Heroes for Hire, Book 8
Dakota's Delight: Heroes for Hire, Book 9
Michael's Mercy (Part of Sleeper SEAL Series)

Tyson's Treasure: Heroes for Hire, Book 10
Jace's Jewel: Heroes for Hire, Book 11
Rory's Rose: Heroes for Hire, Book 12
Brandon's Bliss: Heroes for Hire, Book 13
Liam's Lily: Heroes for Hire, Book 14
North's Nikki: Heroes for Hire, Book 15
Anders's Angel: Heroes for Hire, Book 16
Reyes's Raina: Heroes for Hire, Book 17
Dezi's Diamond: Heroes for Hire, Book 18
Vince's Vixen: Heroes for Hire, Book 19
Ice's Icing: Heroes for Hire, Book 20
Johan's Joy: Heroes for Hire, Book 21
Heroes for Hire, Books 1–3
Heroes for Hire, Books 4–6
Heroes for Hire, Books 7–9
Heroes for Hire, Books 10–12
Heroes for Hire, Books 13–15

SEALs of Steel
Badger: SEALs of Steel, Book 1
Erick: SEALs of Steel, Book 2
Cade: SEALs of Steel, Book 3
Talon: SEALs of Steel, Book 4
Laszlo: SEALs of Steel, Book 5
Geir: SEALs of Steel, Book 6
Jager: SEALs of Steel, Book 7
The Final Reveal: SEALs of Steel, Book 8
SEALs of Steel, Books 1–4
SEALs of Steel, Books 5–8
SEALs of Steel, Books 1–8

The Mavericks
Kerrick, Book 1

Griffin, Book 2
Jax, Book 3
Beau, Book 4
Asher, Book 5
Ryker, Book 6
Miles, Book 7
Nico, Book 8
Keane, Book 9
Lennox, Book 10
Gavin, Book 11
Shane, Book 12

Bullard's Battle Series
Ryland's Reach, Book 1
Cain's Cross, Book 2
Eton's Escape, Book 3
Garret's Gambit, Book 4
Kano's Keep, Book 5
Fallon's Flaw, Book 6
Quinn's Quest, Book 7
Bullard's Beauty, Book 8

Collections
Dare to Be You…
Dare to Love…
Dare to be Strong…
RomanceX3

Standalone Novellas
It's a Dog's Life
Riana's Revenge
Second Chances

Published Young Adult Books:

Family Blood Ties Series

Vampire in Denial
Vampire in Distress
Vampire in Design
Vampire in Deceit
Vampire in Defiance
Vampire in Conflict
Vampire in Chaos
Vampire in Crisis
Vampire in Control
Vampire in Charge
Family Blood Ties Set 1–3
Family Blood Ties Set 1–5
Family Blood Ties Set 4–6
Family Blood Ties Set 7–9
Sian's Solution, A Family Blood Ties Series Prequel
    Novelette

Design series

Dangerous Designs
Deadly Designs
Darkest Designs
Design Series Trilogy

Standalone

In Cassie's Corner
Gem Stone (a Gemma Stone Mystery)
Time Thieves

Published Non-Fiction Books:

Career Essentials

Career Essentials: The Résumé

Career Essentials: The Cover Letter

Career Essentials: The Interview

Career Essentials: 3 in 1